PRAISE FOR

Vendela Vida's

LET THE NORTHERN LIGHTS ERASE YOUR NAME

"What a brilliantly constructed lightning-flash of a novel: compelling, surprising, economical, lush, beautifully written. Reading this book reminded me of how powerful the novel can be—how addictive and vital—and of how rarely a writer as precise, artful, and passionate as Vendela Vida comes along."
                              —George Saunders, author of *In Persuasion Nation*

"'I had hired the new Hungarian florist in town to do the flower arrangement,' the narrator of Vendela Vida's new novel says of her father's funeral. 'A mistake. A ruby banner hung diagonally, like a beauty contestant's sash, across a garish bouquet near the casket. In large silver lettering: BE LOVED.' This tone of dark whimsy suffuses the whole book and accounts for much of its peculiarly biting charm. You've seen it before, in movies like *Little Miss Sunshine* or *The Royal Tenenbaums* and in books like— well, maybe there aren't any other books that walk this very fine line between high-camp comedy and the lyrical seriousness that Vida's title portends: *Let the Northern Lights Erase Your Name.*"
                              —Madison Smartt Bell, *New York Times Book Review*

"Part prayer, part curse, [*Let the Northern Lights Erase Your Name*] is a tightly restrained expression of anger and yearning, a strangled cri de coeur. Across its surface runs a frozen stream of bleak comedy, while tragedy churns underneath."
                              —*Washington Post*

"Since her mother walked out years earlier, Clarissa, the protagonist of Vida's accomplished second novel, must go to Finland to find the stranger who fathered her. . . . Vida perfectly captures the emotional dimension of Clarissa's search, showing that the truth, no matter how pockmarked, is preferable to fiction."
                              —*People*

"Vida's second novel couldn't be released at a better time: It's a quick read with surprising warmth and weight, perfect for a cold January weekend indoors. . . . What may linger most vividly with readers is the gelid beauty of the Lapland setting, evoked nicely in Vida's clean and simple prose." —*Time Out Chicago*

"By the end of this spare, unflinching novel, Vida has successfully gotten away with a provocative assertion: There's no such thing as closure, and sometimes the best way to heal a family is to rip yourself away from it entirely." —*Minneapolis Star Tribune*

"With grace and precision, Vendela Vida explodes the smallest of details and compresses the widest of landscapes. Intimate and sweeping, *Let the Northern Lights Erase Your Name* dazzles like sun on snow." —Sean Wilsey, author of *Oh the Glory of It All*

"This novel's evanescent beauty is contained in prose as cool and crystalline as the ice hotel where Clarissa spends a night."
—*Entertainment Weekly*

"Vida offers precise, revealing details to describe her characters . . . and in Clarissa, Vida has created a complex and not always likable heroine who is driven by loss and confusion. . . . As a feverish Clarissa moves farther into Lapland and into her mother's past, her search becomes more surreal. . . . This impressionistic quality is reminiscent of other surreal literary searches, like Matsuo Basho's *The Narrow Road to the Deep North* and Kazuo Ishiguro's *When We Were Orphans*. In this case, as in those earlier works, the blurring of the line between real and imaginary underscores a larger truth—that any search for a lost person or a buried piece of history is ultimately a search for the self." —*Los Angeles Times Book Review*

"A taut, intricately layered page-turner that looks deeply and fearlessly into matters of profound human concern."
—Michael Cunningham,
Pulitzer Prize–winning author of *The Hours*

"A taut, darkly witty, and galvanizing tale. . . . Brilliantly distilled, blade-sharp, and as dangerously exhilarating as skating in the dark. A fleet yet emotionally suspenseful tale of a burdened childhood and the liberation of the self."
    —*Booklist*

"[Vida] is an assured writer with an exact and vivid voice. . . . The book's solitary, independent heroine and the exotic ancient setting of the book prove transporting. While the story contains surprises, Vida is wise to resist a tidy resolve, a last-minute turn toward faith. . . . A delight."
    —*Philadelphia Inquirer*

"A stirring novel. . . . Secrets, lies, revelations, and the shimmering difficulties of just getting on with life permeate Vendela Vida's second novel. . . . *Let the Northern Lights Erase Your Name* is deceptively slim and easy to read, its intricacy tucked into small phrases and indelible images. . . . [Vida] disguises a world of heartache in brief, matter-of-fact sketches. . . . This book is much darker than her first, but it is as alive and fascinating as the brilliant atmospheric phenomenon of its title."
    —*Chicago Tribune*

LET THE NORTHERN LIGHTS
ERASE YOUR NAME

LET THE NORTHERN LIGHTS ERASE YOUR NAME A Novel

Vendela Vida

HARPER ⬤ PERENNIAL

NEW YORK ● LONDON ● TORONTO ● SYDNEY

HARPER ● PERENNIAL™ is a trademark of HarperCollins Publishers.

HarperCollins books may be purchased for educational, business, or
sales promotional use through our Special Markets Department.

HarperCollins Publishers Ltd
2 Bloor Street East, 20th Floor
Toronto, Ontario, Canada
M4W 1A8

www.harpercollins.ca

Library and Archives Canada Cataloguing in Publication information is
available upon request.

ISBN-13: 978-1-55468-168-6
ISBN-10: 1-55468-168-5

Designed by Sunil Manchikanti
Map by Paul J. Pugliese

Printed and bound in the United States
RRD 10 9 8 7 6 5 4 3 2 1

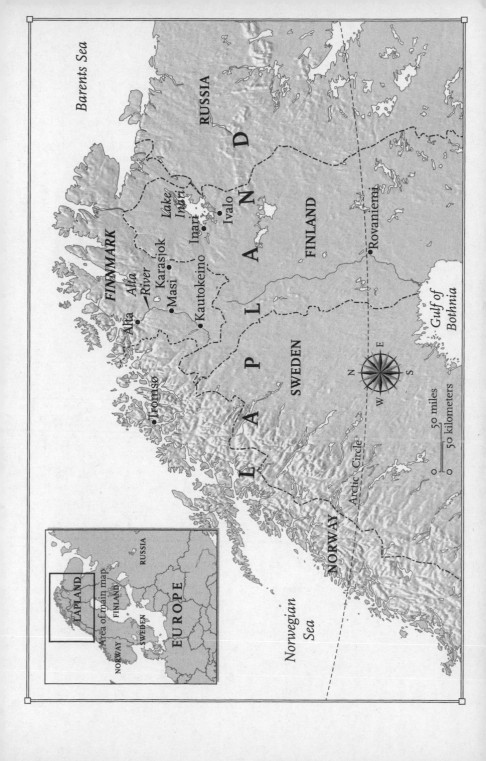

Be Loved

1.

It was three in the afternoon when my plane landed at the Helsinki airport, but outside my window, dusk was already settling in like a bruise. I retrieved my suitcase, its handle cold, and stumbled to the tourist information desk, where a woman with good teeth and bad English helped me find a hotel near the train station. My plan was to take the first train north, to Lapland, after a night of sleep. She directed me toward the hotel's free shuttle bus waiting outside. Its doors opened just as I was preparing to knock.

The blond bus driver's name tag said ARI, but he told me, the only passenger on the bus, that his name was Kari. The name tag belonged to his twin brother, for whom he was filling in (would I please not tell anybody about that, he asked). When it was clear no one else would be boarding, Ari/Kari turned and spoke to the general area where I was sitting. "We go now," he said.

We trailed a snowplow on the road into Helsinki. On the radio, a man's voice sang in English about the pleasures of driving home for Christmas. I asked Kari if he would mind turning it down, and he turned the radio off.

The hotel had three stars on the plaque beneath its name—one star more than I was accustomed to—and I experienced the vacuous pride travelers feel when a choice that's been made for them is a good one. Inside, Kari took my luggage upstairs to reception, at which point, he moved behind the counter to check me in. No-smoking, one night, I told him.

Shortly after I settled into my room, the phone stuttered a staccato cry, far from an American *brrring*. It was Kari telling me he'd be getting off work in an hour. "You like to join me in the lobby for a drink?" he asked.

2.

I said yes, in part out of relief that the call wasn't from Pankaj, my fiancé. My fiancé still? I was no longer sure. Recently, everything around me felt familiar yet amiss, like the first time you ride in the back seat of your own car.

Dad had died a week before I left for Lapland. He was sixty-six, his death unexpected. A heart attack. Pankaj had answered the phone. I was in bed, paying bills, in the Morningside Heights apartment Pankaj and I had shared for nearly five years. He came into the bedroom, tentatively, and knelt on the floor beside me. He did not pray.

"Your father," he said. "Your father."

We left that night for Rhinebeck, where I had grown up. Where Dad had grown up. Where my mother had lived for fifteen years before she disappeared.

3.

I had hired the new Hungarian florist in town to do the flower arrangement. A mistake. A ruby banner hung diagonally, like a beauty contestant's sash, across a garish bouquet near the casket. In large silver lettering: BE LOVED.

The funeral was the first day I envied my brother's ignorance. Since birth, Jeremy has never spoken, so it was unclear whether he understood Dad had died. My family would never acknowledge that Jeremy was retarded; my mother used to say he was slow. She vanished when I was fourteen, Jeremy six. In the hollow months that followed her disappearance, I convinced myself our family was being punished for our silent shame about Jeremy. I said the forbidden word over and over—*retardedretardedretarded*—as though I could undo what was fact: I could unretard him, I could bring my mother home.

While I wiped my tears with my hair—I had forgotten tissues—Jeremy picked at the laces of his dress-up shoes. I bent over, pulled the laces out, and slipped them into my purse. Jeremy was accustomed to Velcro.

A family friend held a reception. Unthawed frozen strawberries, kosher wine, though Dad wasn't Jewish, a woman I had never met sobbing in the corner. Friends and strangers hugged me so tight their chests pushed against mine, alluding to sex, and then vanished. As soon as the last guest had left, the hostess began vacuuming. "All those footprints in the carpet," she said. "They make me tense." I offered to help clean up. She accepted.

Pankaj and I dropped off Jeremy at the Home for Retarded Adults. The main hallway was lined with display cases of women's hats and men's ties. I didn't know why. As I stood below a beret, reporting to the nurse when and what Jeremy had last eaten, Pankaj handed Jeremy a paper bag filled with small plastic bags. The size that wouldn't fit over his head. Jeremy had a thing for plastic bags.

"That was sweet," I said, as we walked to the car. My words didn't match the intensity of my gratitude. From the start, Pankaj had looked out for Jeremy.

We drove back to Dad's house, where we had been staying since we got the phone call. We had left a few lights on, and as we approached the front door, I half-imagined it had been a hoax. Dad was alive and waiting to surprise us. I unlocked the door. "Hello," I called out.

Pankaj started a fire in the living room. I stared at his large lips and his gray-black eyes, the color of papaya seeds. They were framed by long eyelashes, the kind that old ladies on trains made a fuss over. Pankaj could bat them like a flirtatious girl and somehow look virile, handsome, strong.

But tonight his eyes were tunnel-dark, his eyelashes fey. He was moving slowly, the way you would around a predator you didn't want to enrage. I escaped to my father's study.

The study had been my mother's. She claimed to be working on her dissertation on the environmental battles of indigenous peoples. It was her research that initially took her to Lapland in her late twenties. While there, she'd gotten *sidetracked*—that was her word, her explanation. She would sequester herself in the study for a few hours every afternoon, ostensibly writing, but there was a silent understanding in our house that her dissertation would never be finished.

I sat down in Dad's leather chair and opened the drawers of his desk—her desk. I found his address book. Inside, under our last name, Iverton, there were no entries. This was odd: Dad had written me once a month since I'd moved out. Scribbled in miniature handwriting, his letters had described landscaping projects he was working on, or summarized, in too much detail, a film he had recently seen.

I found myself in the ABC section, under "Clar." My mother had named me Clarissa, but Dad never called me by my full name. Penned into the book were four addresses for me: one P.O. box in college, one address in Lexington, Kentucky, two in Manhattan. He had entered my new address each time I'd moved and never crossed out the old one. I tried to imagine me living in each of these apartments, carrying on four different lives at once. In my Kentucky life, would my father be dead?

I didn't recognize the majority of names. I assumed these were the owners of homes he had helped landscape. Why hadn't more of his clients shown up for the funeral? The service had been small.

I sorted through the drawers—old bills, letters postmarked in the early nineties, sea glass, owner's manuals to appliances we no longer owned. In the bottom drawer, I found a large manila envelope that appeared not to have been opened more than once or twice. CLARISSA'S was written on the outside. She had been gone for fourteen years, but I immediately recognized my mother's handwriting. Her *S*'s were exuberant, forward-leaning *8*'s.

I shook the contents out onto the desk: grade-school report cards, notes from teachers commenting on my shyness in class. I didn't recall this about myself, and was surprised and strangely embarrassed—we like to remember our childhoods a certain way. I sorted through watercolors—"age 7" written in one corner—a note to the tooth fairy, a photo of me in front of the Washington Monument, wearing a dress patterned with keys.

Beneath a dried leaf, splitting at its stem, I found my birth certificate. I had never seen it before. I read it and read it again. I turned it over. With my forearm, I swept everything else on the desk into a far corner. Papers and a desk calendar dropped to the floor. I moved the certificate to the center of the desk and I read it again.

4.

Pankaj found me sitting on the shower floor, still wearing my bra and black stockings. He stood, blurry, on the other side of the clear door. The birth certificate was in his hand. "Do you want to talk?" he said.

I shook my head. I was emptying the bottles of Dad's dandruff shampoo, like tar, down the drain. Pankaj carefully placed the birth certificate inside the cover of a book about Vargas girls; it had been sitting above the toilet since he had given it to Dad the previous Christmas. Inside, I knew the inscription read: "To Richard, my future father-in-law. With admiration, Pankaj." Pankaj took off his clothes, opened the shower door, and sat next to me on the tiled floor.

"The water's colder when you're sitting," he said, and reached up to adjust the temperature. He picked up the blue bar of soap, Dad's soap, and rubbed it under my armpits. He took my Dad's other, non-dandruff shampoo, and washed my hair. We sat in the shower so long the water turned tepid. Pankaj stood up, stepped out, and held a towel open for me.

I crawled out of the shower, and Pankaj bent over and rolled off my stockings and unhooked my bra. He wrapped me in the towel and picked me up. I couldn't raise my arms around his neck or help in any way.

He carried me into my childhood bedroom, which had not changed: twin beds, a Sears stereo, and a hundred tiny holes in the wall where I'd thumbtacked my album covers. Pankaj put a blanket over me, tucking it in like he was making a bed. Then he left the room.

I stared at a photo of my father on the bookshelf. His arms like a game-show host, displaying a washer and dryer he bought when I was fifteen. Laundry had been my mother's job, one that we both resisted taking on when she was gone. He had believed the new machines would make her absence less obvious. It had been my favorite picture of my father, but now it seemed to belong to some other teenager.

Pankaj returned.

"He should have told me," I said to his silhouette.

"He was protecting you. He—"

"He was a liar."

Pankaj was holding a bowl and a spoon.

"Applesauce," he said. "It's all that was in the fridge."

"Didn't anyone bring anything over?" I asked. "Isn't that what people do?"

"Sorry," he said.

"Sorry?" I said. "What are you sorry about? You're the only one who doesn't have anything to apologize for."

He didn't answer, and, at the time, I took this as a sign of modesty. We both twisted into the same twin bed.

A few hours later, I learned why he was sorry.

"Are you awake?" he said.

I nodded and then said yes.

"I knew."

"You knew what?"

"I knew about Richard. That he wasn't your real dad."

In the dark, I tried to see Pankaj's mouth.

"How long have you known?" I said. I spoke slowly. I didn't want any room for misinterpretation.

"A long time."

"Like days?"

"Longer. Since we were—"

"Engaged?" I said.

"Teenagers."

"What?"

He said nothing.

"How?"

"Your mom told me."

"What? Why?"

"Well, let me think about what happened."

Pankaj was stalling, preparing a lie.

"Don't make me wait."

"Your mom told my mom."

"Fifteen years ago?"

"About that time."

"Fifteen years! Almost half my life. More than half my life."

Pankaj exhaled.

"So everybody knows? Dad knew? My mom? You, Gita? Gita! Your fucking mom knows who my real fucking father is and I don't? What the fuck is this? Does the fucking florist who can't even fucking spell know?"

"No."

"Really, Pankaj. Was this posted at the train station?"

"I didn't want to know. I wish I didn't."

"Fuck you," I said. "And tonight was the right time to tell me?"

"I'm sorry," he said. "I guess I felt deceitful, with you in the shower like that. I thought it would make things easier if I told you I knew. Later, you would never forgive me."

I switched on the bedside lamp. I stood up, stared at the bookshelf, pulled at the spine of my first-year Russian textbook and threw it to the floor. The carpet absorbed its thud. I had wanted thunder.

"Of all days to tell me," I said, and threw down another book, this one a dictionary, unabridged.

"Stop saying that," Pankaj yelled, "and stop with the books."

"You and Dad are the same. When you don't tell someone something like that, you are fucking with their life."

"I understand how you must feel," he said. He was sitting up in bed. He was wearing one of Dad's old sweatshirts.

"Take that off," I said.

"I'm sorry. I didn't pack well." He removed the sweatshirt, folded it neatly, and placed it on the bedside table.

"First of all, you do not understand how I feel. So take that back."

"You're right. I don't know, but I can imagine ..."

"Imagine! You can't imagine anything. Has every person you know been betraying you for fifteen years?"

"Not everyone knows—"

"Shut up. Has everyone close to you—your father, your fiancé, your who-the-fuck-knows been lying to you? Answer me."

"No," he said. He stood to comfort me.

"Stay away," I said. I pulled an old doll off the shelf and held it between us.

He stared at the doll, as though addressing her. "I know you're angry with me right now."

"You're a genius, really. Not only at philosophy, but at emotions. You know that I'm angry with you. Wow."

"What can I do for you?" he said. "I think you need some sleep. Everything will be better in the morning." He looked scared.

"Really? Will Dad not be dead in the morning? Will my fiancé not be a liar? Will it turn out tomorrow morning that not everyone betrayed me? Ah! Morning!"

"Please stop saying that word," Pankaj said.

"Morning?"

"Stop saying *betrayed*. You make it sound like—"

"Like what? Like I was betrayed?"

"Please go to sleep. Everything will be better tomorrow. I promise."

"You promise?" I said. I was now holding the doll to my chest. It was an ugly doll. I didn't know where it had come from or why I had kept it. "I suppose I should be happy now that I know, right? Dad was a cuckold. And I have a fucking father in fucking Finland."

"He wasn't a cuckold," Pankaj said. "You were born before your mom met Richard."

I sat down on the floor.

"Where does the word *cuckold* come from, anyway?" Pankaj said.

"I don't know but I think you're right. This is a good time for an etymological discussion. While we're at it, why don't we figure out where *asshole* comes from? Where *get out of my room* comes from."

"I was trying to change the subject," he said. His voice cracked like a boy's. "Listen, I'm going to go downstairs for a little bit. I'll be there if you need anything." He headed toward the door. His chest looked hairier than usual, his legs skinnier.

"Is there anything else you have to tell me?" I said. "Any other surprises? If so, tell me now. I'm serious. I should know everything and get it over with."

"No," he said.

"No what?"

"No more surprises," Pankaj said. "I'm sorry."

"Please leave," I said.

"Do you care if I come back here to sleep, to check up on you? I don't want to sleep in your dad's room." He gestured toward the sweatshirt.

"I don't care what you do. Just leave. And don't sleep in my dad's bed. Or whoever the fuck he is."

Pankaj closed the door. I went to bed and took the ugly doll with me.

5.

When I woke, it was still dark. I stared at the person sleeping in the twin bed next to mine. *There must be someone else,* I thought. *There must be someone I'm closer to.* I made my way to the bathroom and sat on the toilet but couldn't pee. I curled over so my eyes were pressed to my knees. I stared at the floor. I picked up a piece of dental floss that had missed the garbage can and tossed it in.

Dad's red, white, and blue headband hung from the bathroom doorknob. A John McEnroe fan, Dad wore the headband whenever he worked in the garden, his gray hair rising up from the top like exhaust. I sniffed the headband—it smelled of soil—and put it on my head.

I was seven when my mother was pregnant with Jeremy. After her water broke, she called a babysitter to spend the night with me. The babysitter, Tara, was seventeen. She wore a low-cut shirt and, as she leaned over to help me with my Peter Pan coloring book, I could see the tattoo of an eagle spanning her braless breasts. In red crayon, she scribbled the word *fag* above Peter Pan's head.

"When your parents come home, they'll bring your new brother or sister to meet you," she said. "Isn't that exciting?"

I nodded.

But when my parents came home, my new brother, Jeremy, wasn't with them. My father and mother retreated to their bedroom early. I could hear my mother's sobs through the door, and Dad's murmurs of comfort. I tried to enter their bedroom, but the door was locked—it had never been locked before—and I was left standing in the hallway, staring at the repeating reflection of myself in the faceted glass doorknob.

The next day, in the car on the way to the hospital, my mother turned to me. "I almost forgot to tell you," she said. "Your brother was born with something wrong with him."

"Will he get better?" I asked.

"No, he'll be that way his whole life," she said.

I caught Dad's eye in the rearview mirror. He stared at me until my mother, who was sitting in the passenger seat, readjusted the mirror so she could see her reflection.

———

I didn't open the door to Dad's bedroom. I didn't want to know if he had made the bed that morning, his last morning.

I walked downstairs and turned on the radio. Dad had it set to jazz. Behind the couch stood two globes. I spun the older, more expensive one around so fast it rattled on its stand. Then I found Dad's toolbox and, using a saw, I cut the globe loose from its brass arm, holding it at a tilt. It fell to the floor, and I kicked it like a soccer ball. It split into three large pieces. Nothing was inside.

I stepped out into the garden, now shaded in dark hues and snow. Our bird feeder swung from a branch, jostled by wind. For over a decade now, it had been hanging from a coat hanger—a temporary solution that, like many, had endured. I moved a deck chair beneath the tree. I took the bird feeder down, seeds falling on me like wedding rice.

6.

At seven, I opened the door to my room and stared at Pankaj. I would leave him, I decided. After this was over, in a week or a month, I would travel to Missoula or Memphis and find a man who fixed planes or raced horses and didn't need love, who hadn't loved anyone. He and I would kiss over dinner with pizza in our mouths. He and I would know no one else in the world.

I slipped into the narrow bed where Pankaj was sleeping and rested my cheek on the edge of the pillow. I felt him stirring.

I'm going to leave you, I thought.

"Don't you ever leave me," I whispered.

7.

The next morning, we drove back to the city in silence. In my lap, I held an ice tray. I pressed ice against my eyes to stop the swelling. When a cube began melting, I would throw it in the backseat, then extract a new, colder one from the tray.

In the coming nights, Pankaj slept on the couch; I slept in our bedroom, with a wicker laundry hamper in front of the door. I had first intended the hamper to block the door, but that had proven to be a nuisance—I'd had to move it, stuffed and overflowing with unwashed clothes, every time I needed to go to the bathroom.

But I left the hamper two feet from the entrance. If Pankaj came into the bedroom, he would ask, "What's this for?"

"To hamper you," I would say.

8.

But Pankaj hadn't once tried to come into the bedroom. Instead, he spent the first few hours of each night sitting outside the bedroom door, explaining to me how he didn't think what he'd done was wrong. Why I shouldn't be hurt. How I was in shock from Dad's death, from what I'd learned.

The phone rang less than usual. "Everyone's trying to give you space," Pankaj said. *Cowards, all of them,* I thought, *trying to spare themselves.*

Pankaj's mother, Gita, called.

"Not a chance," I said.

Pankaj had been three years ahead of me in high school, and his mother and my mother had been close—for a while. Every relationship with my mother came with an expiration date.

Gita was a short, round woman who had studied classical dance in India. She had once been beautiful, and at sixty, still flirted her way out of parking tickets, middle seats on airplanes, a vase that slipped from her fingers at a crystal store. When I was fourteen, she showed me her swami closet—a linen closet in her upstairs hallway, where she kept photos of her ancestors. Every morning, she told me, she would honor the dead, and when she was done, ring a small bell. I had always loved Gita. I had wished she was my mother, even before mine was gone.

The fourth or fifth time she called, Pankaj pleaded with me to talk to her.

"She was in on it, too," I said to the door between us.

"You're acting like this was a conspiracy," he said. "Please. My mother cares about you."

"Your mother also cares about ringing a fucking bell every morning. Who does she think she is? Big Ben?"

Silence. He mumbled something to his mother and hung up.

"I never knew you could be so nasty," he said. "You made her cry."

"Boo hoo hoo," I said.

9.

I had to wait three days for a passport, my first. Otherwise, I would have left immediately.

Each night that I was sequestered, Pankaj pushed an article or two under the bedroom door. This was something he did—he searched through the Hunter College library and photocopied articles he thought I might like. Never was the copy too dark or too light, never was a marginal letter cut off. He'd staple each article and keep it stored unbent and unsullied in a folder until he got it to me. So much thought was put into a staple; its placement was always diagonal, its grasp tight. The articles were usually in reference to something we'd talked about. The last one had been about the elephant sculpture in front of the UN. Its penis was so large they covered it with a shrub.

Now, in the days after Dad's funeral, Pankaj tried to coax me to read articles about grieving, about shock. He slid them under the door; I ignored them. On the night before I left for Finland, Pankaj sat outside, pleading with me to read something he'd copied from a philosophy journal. "I think it might help you understand your mother," he said.

I pulled out two loud-ticking alarm clocks I'd come across when furtively packing, and held one clock up to each ear. All I could hear was time.

10.

I left our apartment at six a.m., passing Pankaj sleeping on the couch, his right foot extended on the coffee table. No one knew I was going anywhere. Disappearing is nothing. I learned this from my mother.

11.

The desk in my Helsinki hotel room had a thin phone book in its top drawer. Finland was so small that every listing fit into the same volume, the numbers organized by town. I flipped to the town of Inari and scanned the names until I got to "Valkeapää." He was listed. I shut the phone book and flossed my teeth. I found the number again and dialed. A man answered, and I hung up.

I showered in sulfur-smelling water. The shower floor was the same surface, same elevation, as that of the rest of the bathroom, but with a drain. I washed my hair with hotel shampoo—miniature bottles that pictured warmer landscapes. The towels were too small. I sniffed the clothes I'd worn during travel, found they had the plane smell of Band-Aids, and dressed in corduroy pants, a blouse, and two sweaters.

Nobody in the world knows where I am. I felt like a bank robber, safe in Mexico. A minute later: *Nobody in the world could find me if they wanted to.* I felt unworthy of being sought.

I turned on the television, using the remote, though the room was so narrow I sat two feet away from the small screen. I settled on a Berenstain Bears cartoon dubbed in Finnish. It was impressive how closely the mouth movements of the Bears seemed to match the dubbed words. Finnish, apparently, was the Bears' native language.

I have some experience in these matters. I perfect subtitles for a small company called Soutitre. The films that come to me have usually been shoddily translated and are full of anachronistic language ("But madam, I love thee") and literal interpretations ("My heart is a rotten plum"). I don't have to speak the original language. My job is to make sure the English translation is smooth, the grammar correct.

I get paid by the minute. Eight dollars. For a ninety-minute film, $720; for two hours, $960. I am forever counting.

12.

At six, I descended to the lobby in the glass elevator. Kari was standing on the first floor, and my instinct upon seeing him was to push the button for the fifth floor and call the meeting off. But he had seen me. He was waiting, with a cup of something in each hand.

"Hello," he said, but it sounded like *how low?*

Good question.

He offered me one of the cups. "*Glögi*. It's a holiday drink."

"What's in it?" I asked, sniffing. The cup was warm in my palms.

"It's hot wine."

I found the gesture sweet, charming even, until, looking past him into the reception area, I spotted a table where it was being given out for free. I took a sip, then another. Warmth rose to my face, to my ears.

Kari said I looked nice and asked if I had showered.

"Yes," I said, and added, "it was a long trip."

I didn't clean up for you.

"I was thinking," he said, "that we go somewhere else, not the hotel bar."

I shrugged and said that I'd like to get out, see a little bit of Helsinki. I had only one night there.

"Yes, thank you for understanding. I don't want anyone at the hotel to think I'm hitting you."

"Hitting me?"

"Yes," Kari said. "Let me think where we go." He put his fist under his wide chin to prove that he was thinking.

"I know a place," Kari said. He smiled.

We walked outside and I paused—something like blood had been shed on the cobblestone street.

"I guess some people don't like the *glögi* so much," Kari said.

The sky was moonless, black, the street crowded with

people. So late and so many. And then I realized it was only six o'clock.

We walked to an intersection, where Kari paused and looked around, as though trying to figure out the direction of the wind. We proceeded down the hill and toward the gray bay shaped like a fist. He stopped at one point to run into a Diesel clothing store. I waited outside, surprised by the volume of techno blaring from the building. He didn't ask me to come in. I assumed he was getting directions.

The cold on my ears was sudden and burning. I pulled up the hood of my parka. It was, like all hats and hoods, too big for my small head. I had no peripheral vision.

"This way," Kari said, emerging from the store. We passed *glögi* stands that appeared to have been set up for the Christmas season, and an improbable number of hair salons and bars that looked alike, all lined with shelves of backlit bottles. Red tulips stood in the window of every store. There wasn't a poinsettia in sight.

As we walked, Kari became no more and no less interesting. He was at school, studying to be a pharmacist. His parents lived up north. His brother was currently on vacation in Greece. "I'm a winter widow," he said.

I must have looked surprised.

"My girlfriend's studying in Holland," he explained.

We walked in silence for a moment. Two young women without coats ran out of a parked car and into a bar. Their arms were crossed over their chests, at nipple line.

"What are you doing here?" Kari asked. His inflection was misplaced; his question sounded like an accusation.

"I'm a real winter widow," I said. "My fiancé and his family, they all died."

"I'm sorry," Kari said.

"It's okay," I said. "It was their time."

13.

Travel is made for liars. Or liars are made by travel.

I had given a different explanation to the Belgian deejay sitting next to me on the flight from New York to Brussels. She grated on my nerves, and I wasn't sure why. She was too eager, too loud, and I decided I could be mean to her. "Do you think that's the Great Lakes?" she asked, looking over me and out the window.

Two hours earlier, we had departed eastward out of Kennedy.

"Yes," I said. "I'm quite sure that's the Great Lakes."

I turned my head into my pillow and closed my eyes. Minutes later, she tapped me on the shoulder. "You are sleeping?" she asked.

She woke me up a second time as the duty-free cart squeezed through the main cabin. She wanted to make sure I was up, in case there was something I wanted to buy; she recommended a certain face cream.

"It do you wonder," she said, squinting at my forehead.

After the cart had passed and the deejay had made her purchases, she asked why I was going to Finland.

I told her that the man I had called Dad had recently passed away, and I'd discovered that my mother—who disappeared when I was fourteen—had lied to me. As a result, I'd spent my life deceived about the identity of my father. My birth certificate said that my real father was the man she'd been married to before. He was a Sami priest in Lapland. I was going to find him. When I finished my story, I made a gesture like I had jumped out of a cake. "Ta-da," I said.

We didn't talk the rest of the trip. A shame. She probably thought I had made the story up.

At passport control, I handed over my landing card. "Purpose of your visit?" said the man behind the counter.

"Business," I said. "I'm here on business."

14.

I looked to my left, where I expected to see Kari, but he wasn't there. At one point in our walk, he must have turned. I circled around in place until I felt a hand on my elbow. "Didn't you see me?" he said. I shook my head no, my hood swinging left and right.

I hadn't been touched by anyone since Pankaj, the liar, had tried to comfort me. Kari saw my eyes on his hand and let go.

"Sorry," he said.

I forced myself to smile. "About what?"

I was impressed by his choice of a bar. It was on a back-street, and from the outside, it looked candlelit, warm. Inside, groups of friends convened around blond wood tables bordered by benches. Plum-colored tulips were mixed with red berries and placed in the center of each table.

Kari gave his last name to the hostess. It sounded short but looked long when she wrote it down. The plans had evidently changed to include dinner. I didn't mind—I had a night to kill. Another woman escorted us to the bar's wooden stools. A third came by for our coats.

I gave her mine, along with my hat and scarf, and then shivered.

"Why do you do that?" Kari asked.

"What?"

"What you just did ... what do you call it?" He imitated me, doing an exaggerated shudder.

I told him it was called shivering.

"But that's not real," he said.

"Not real? You mean not natural."

"Yes, it's not natural. You don't *sliver* because you're cold."

I shivered again.

Kari had changed clothes since driving the bus. He was wearing a black-and-white speckled sweater that made me sad. All that effort put into making something so ugly.

"How old are you?" I asked.

"Twenty-three," he said. He was adding a few years. "And you?"

"Twenty-six," I lied, subtracting.

Kari ordered a rum and coke. I ordered a vodka and cranberry.

We knocked glasses, and I studied Kari's face. He had pale, doughy skin. I could see the palimpsest of teenage acne.

I took another look around the bar, at the woman who'd written down his last name, whatever it was. She was wearing camouflage pants and was admiring another waitress's camouflage belt. Gone were the deep-jungle patterns of the eighties; these were sand-colored, period-specific. Fashion knows no bounds.

Kari and I had nothing to say to each other.

I told him an anecdote that had amused Pankaj:

One night, when I'd first moved to New York and gotten a job waitressing at a steak house, I had a table of Swedes. After they'd finished their food, I asked the busboy, Gilbert, to clear the table. Gilbert was from Guatemala and kept a picture of his wife wrapped around the handle of his comb. The picture was so frayed that the one time he'd shown it to me, I couldn't make out much of her appearance except that, in the photo, she seemed to be wearing something red. He sent her money every month.

I paused to ask Kari if he understood everything so far.

He nodded, and I continued:

Gilbert returned from the table and told me that each time he tried to clear their plates, the Swedes had laughed.

"I'm sure they're not laughing at you," I told him. "Go try again."

I watched as Gilbert returned to the table. He asked if they were done, and the Swedes said something to him and then laughed. He came back to my side, confused. "See?" he said.

This time, I went to the table. "Is something wrong?" I asked. The man who was leaning forward in his chair, the man who had sent back his steak because it was overcooked, decided to answer my question. "Your busboy keeps coming to the table and asking, 'You Finnish?' and we say, 'No, we're Swedish.'"

Kari stared at me. Pankaj had liked this story so much he had told it a couple times himself.

A minute passed. Kari downed his drink, examined his knuckles. At last, he spoke. "Why did the busboy think they were Finnish?"

15.

My mother's friendship with Gita, Pankaj's mother, bore a strong resemblance to that of schoolgirls—they would talk on the phone every night, rehashing the day's events. For a short time, Dad and Pankaj's father became friends as well, drawn in by their wives' enthusiasm for each other.

One night, my parents and Pankaj's parents went out to dinner together, leaving Pankaj and me at his house with a pack of ramen noodles and a salad. School had started a month before—I was a freshman; he was a senior. We had never exchanged more than a few words before, but I had watched him from afar. I knew the location of his locker, I knew he brushed his teeth after lunch.

Pankaj took me into the living room and told me his family had recently remodeled. I said it was nice, though it looked sterile. There was a fresh bouquet of yellow flowers on the coffee table, and Pankaj said his father had In Full Bloom, an upscale florist, send his mother an arrangement every week. That impressed me as much as it was supposed to.

We sat on the couch. I had been instructed to remove my shoes upon entering the house, and I tried to look casual and quick as I lifted my bare feet to rest on the glass coffee table. But my heels fell against the surface harder than I'd intended, and the glass shattered and collapsed beneath their weight. Only the metal legs remained.

Pankaj shot up.

"Oh my God," I said. "I'm so sorry." I reached for the tilted flower vase. The water was spilling, the petals scattering.

"What were you thinking?" Pankaj asked.

"I didn't know it was so fragile," I said.

"It's *glass.*"

"I'm sorry, but there must have been a crack. I remember seeing one." I was standing now, too. "My mom—she'll be so pissed."

"*Your* mom?" Pankaj said.

"We need a garbage can. And a vacuum," I said. I was holding the vase in front of me, as if offering it to him.

"Are you okay?" he asked.

I looked down. "Yeah, I think so."

"What time is it?" he asked.

"Six something. Maybe not even that. We got here before six."

"Let's go," Pankaj said. "I know where they bought the table."

Pankaj drove a green station wagon. My seat belt felt too tight, but I didn't want to adjust it. My big toe was bleeding, and I brought my right foot up to my left knee to examine it.

Pankaj looked over. "Shoot."

"It doesn't hurt," I said, though suddenly it did.

Pankaj asked to speak to the manager of the furniture store. I had never asked for a manager.

"You're in luck," the manager said. He had another table exactly like the one I'd broken. He walked us to it.

"I don't have that kind of money," I whispered to Pankaj.

"I have a credit card," he said.

"I'll pay you back," I said, and he nodded. I knew I would have to ask Dad for the money. It would be our secret from my mother.

We carried the table out to Pankaj's car, stopping twice when I needed to adjust my hands. At his house, we picked up the glass and placed the pieces in a garbage bag Pankaj had lined with paper bags. "Careful," he said, as I got to the smaller shards. We vacuumed. The old table's legs had left small circles in the carpet, and we matched the new table's legs to the indents. I placed the vase of yellow flowers in the center of the table.

At nine, when our parents returned, Pankaj and I were sitting on the couch, watching TV. Pankaj had found a Band-Aid for my foot.

"How was dinner?" Gita asked.

"Good," I said. We had forgotten to eat.

———

Pankaj graduated from high school that spring. I didn't talk to him again until nine years later, when I was living in New York. One Saturday, a friend took me to a party in Brooklyn. I didn't know the hosts. I walked in and saw Pankaj standing by a birthday cake.

"Happy birthday," I said.

"It's not my birthday," he said. "I play in the band."

Pankaj played the sitar. I danced in a cluster with Pankaj's older sister, Archana, and her friends, all of them tall. Other women formed other clusters around us. The men stood by the tables of drinks. It was spring and hot in the loft, and I loved it all—the heat, Pankaj's sister, and the loudness of the music, which was not good.

Within four months, Pankaj and I moved in together. After two months of living together, we were in love. Despair was a thing of the past, discarded like a scarf through the window of a moving car.

———

After we'd been together three years, Pankaj got a position teaching philosophy at Hunter College. He was working on his dissertation. I quit waitressing and started my subtitling job at

Soutitre. I was happy there, but I knew that I would soon have to move on—there was no promotion to be had, no position I coveted. The company was a way station for Czech and Swiss and German expatriates needing a reason to stay in New York for a few years. But what was my excuse? I had no excuse.

Years passed, and I was still working at Soutitre, and Pankaj was still finishing his dissertation on free will. The stagnation in our separate and joined lives prompted Pankaj to propose. Atlantic City. He'd lost fifty dollars at blackjack. I'd won three hundred quarters on a Yosemite Sam slot.

At the end of the night, we took the elevator up to our room. Somewhere around the twenty-fourth floor, Pankaj got down on both knees. I thought he had fallen.

16.

Kari and I got our dinner at the bar.

"So why are you here only one night?" Kari asked.

I told him I was going to Lapland.

"Which part?"

"Finnish Lapland," I said. "Around Inari."

"You're going to see some Sami," Kari said. "They're like your, what do you call the people who wear feathers? Indian?"

"Native American."

In my guidebook, I had read about discrimination against the Sami, that they'd become Finnish or Swedish or Norwegian citizens only within the last generation.

"My parents work at tourist agency for ski area in the north," Kari said. "One year they can't open the ski ride because a Sami man said his reindeer likes to eat there. He said the reindeer was there first. That stupid reindeer made everyone lose much money."

Kari picked the cherry out of his drink and made a slow production of biting it off its stem. This was supposed to be sensual.

"You know how you can tell a Sami?" he offered. "They're short and they walk with their legs like this." Kari got up from his bar stool and stood bowlegged.

"Sit down," I said. He did.

"This is because they hang their babies from sacks on the wall and that's how their legs grow. And typical, they are darker and shorter than other Scandinavians."

I stared past Kari.

My mother had light hair, even before she dyed it lighter. I had black eyes (like Dad's—or so I had believed), hair the color of bark, and at five foot three, I was four inches shorter than my mother. I knew her height from the missing-person report Dad had had to fill out. From the top of the stairway, I'd listened as he'd told the detectives: "Olivia Ann Iverton ... a hundred and thirty-five pounds, five foot seven ... People who have reason to be upset with her? Where do I start?"

17.

Our third round of drinks arrived. I was drinking to keep awake. Kari looked toward the television above the bar. I strained my head to see what he was watching. Some sport.

"Handball," Kari explained. "I play it, too. I'm good."

I asked, stupidly, if it was a hard sport.

"Oh, yes," he said, tucking his dirty-blond hair behind his ears. "Men who play are very strong. Good athletes."

We watched the handball game in silence. "Not an exciting game, this one," Kari said, turning his attention back to me.

"What do you want to do next?" he asked.

"What are our options?" I pictured myself lying in my hotel-room bed, alone, dark shadows crowding my head.

Kari turned in his chair so his legs were on either side of mine. "You know what our options are," he said, and pressed my legs together. I fought my reflex to press outward. I had terrible taste in flings.

"And don't worry," he added, now tightening his knees' grip on mine. "I picked something up when I went into the Diesel store."

I tried to think what it could be—a hat? a vest? a better-looking sweater?

"They give out free condoms there." He opened his hand like a magician at the end of a trick, displaying his surprise. "I learned from last time I was with someone like you."

"Like me?"

"Yeah," he said. "Enough like you. She wasn't American, she was Finnish."

I laughed in his face.

"Ready?" he asked.

I nodded. I needed to leave.

When the check came, we split it. From his pocket, Kari pulled out a folded but crisp five-euro bill and left it for the bartender. It was the same bill I had given Kari earlier, when he had driven me to the hotel. I was glad to see him get rid of it. It felt wrong to go to bed with a man who had your tip in his pocket.

18.

"No one else is on this floor," Kari said as I unlocked the door to my room. "I made sure you were private."

I stepped into the room and was again surprised by how small it was. Kari sat on the bed and handed me one of the two beers he'd brought up from the refrigerator behind the reception desk. He drank his quickly. He got up to pee; when he returned, he reeked of beer and urine.

I checked the closets for a blanket. I stood on tiptoes to reach the top shelf. A force came from behind me, and at first, I thought I was falling. Kari's hands were below my ribs, and he was lifting me. When I pulled the blanket out from the shelf, it fell to the floor—I wasn't prepared for its weight.

Kari sat down on the bed with me in his lap. He cupped a hand over my breast and blew into my ear. He removed his hand from my breast and stuck two fingers into my mouth. *Bite,* I thought. I fought the instinct and sucked on his wide fingers. They tasted like coins.

He pushed me onto the bed, his belt buckle digging into my belly. I peeled off his sweater and shirt. He tugged my blouse over my head, scratching my nose with the second button.

He flipped me over onto my stomach and traced my spine; I knew he would. It surprises everyone, the dark hair that lines the center of my back. I've had it since I was fourteen and underweight. *Lunago,* the doctors called it—the same fur that lines a fetus's body in the womb.

Everything I knew about my body I had learned from the four men I'd been with. I knew that my nipples were large for such small breasts. That my flat stomach was my best feature. That my arms were shapeless. If someone told me they liked my arms, I knew they were lying.

Kari was no longer touching me. I assumed he was masturbating.

I rolled over on my back and looked at him. His face was pale. He put his head on my breast, suckled at a spot a few inches away from my nipple, and then bounded off the bed and into the bathroom. He didn't bother closing the door.

He threw up twice—once near the toilet, once inside. A part of me was relieved that what had started had ended. I tried not to act too cheerful as I filled a glass with water from the sink. I held it out to him, and he knocked it away.

He passed out on his stomach, one hand on the base of the toilet. I removed a sheet from the bed and draped it over him.

I was tempted to call the front desk. "He's one of yours," I'd say.

I could leave, but where would I go?

I considered calling Virginia. I hadn't told her I was going to Lapland, that I was going anywhere at all. Virginia and I had become friends in high school, drawn together by our unconventional home lives. I had a mother who had vanished; Virginia's mom lived with two men and was romantically involved with both. When we were fifteen, I gave Virginia a key to my house, which she wore around her neck the way coaches wear whistles. She lost her virginity on our front lawn, as I stood guard from my bedroom window.

But at some point, Virginia and I had switched places; she had become the responsible one. She now worked as a counselor at a clinic for abused women. Her husband was a doctor who operated on children with cleft palates. Together they traveled to Africa every year, as part of a project called Operation Smile.

I knew she would tell Pankaj where I was, so I had told her nothing. People assume those in mourning aren't thinking clearly. Ha! My brain was a razor. A flesh-eating predator.

I pulled the hotel desk chair close to the television and turned it on, the volume off. I held the remote in my hand but leaned forward to change the channels on the TV itself—Bill

Cosby talking about nutrition, an interview with an amputee—and eventually found what I knew was an Italian movie with Finnish subtitles. I'd worked on the English subtitles for this film. Usually, I can't bear to look at a project I've worked on after it's done, but this morning was different. I knew the lines the actress was saying, and, in my head, I recited the English translation of her accusations. She was angry for five minutes, ten minutes. She was angry for most of the film. Though the volume was still turned off, when she screamed, I, too, opened my mouth. We screamed silently together.

Because I Was Late

1.

The last time I saw my mother was on December 16, 1990. I was fourteen.

Behind the doors of my advent calendar: a harp. I was on winter break from school—Jeremy, too. My mother was taking us upstate, to Albany, to see a friend from California named Fern. After a twenty-year silence, Fern had written my mother a Christmas card, and a plan for us to visit had been hatched.

That morning, Dad went out to the car to warm it up—something he did for my mother in winter. His primary concern was her comfort. In the summer, he'd go out to the car to start the air-conditioning.

I lured Jeremy to the Subaru with a laundry basket filled with clean balled-up socks—he liked to unball them. Dad saluted Jeremy (Jeremy didn't like physical affection), and kissed me good-bye on my forehead. Then he kissed my mother on the forehead, too. I hated that he did that; I wanted my mother to be special. I vowed that the next time he tried to kiss my forehead, I'd duck.

2.

In preceding weeks, my mother had been unusually affection-
ate toward me. I wasn't sure how long it would last, her warmth,
so I followed it like a sunbather at dusk, chasing the sun.

Five minutes into the drive, my mother slid a book on tape
into the stereo. It was a four-cassette biography of Margaret
Mead. I listened, I waited. When the first tape ended, I ejected
it and placed it back in the box. I had been preparing a subject my mother might be interested in. "What was Fern like?" I
asked. "When you were growing up?"

"Oh," she said. "She was never ambitious. I think her parents' divorce screwed her up. I remember how much earwax
she had in her ears. Yellow, though, not red. Or black. Or
whatever. Earwax gets out of control when a kid's parents go
through a divorce. You know, a sign of neglect."

And with that, she inserted the second Margaret Mead tape.

3.

We pulled into Fern's driveway. My mother used the rearview mirror to apply lipstick. "How do I look?" she asked, and
turned toward me.

"Beautiful." It was true, but I regretted saying it. I was love-
sick.

I immediately disliked Fern. The makeup on her face was
several tones too dark for her skin. It emphasized the deep

lines that extended above and below the edges of her lips. My mother complimented Fern on her blue sweater.

"I got my colors done last month," Fern said.

"Well, they did a good job."

"Your mother," Fern said, still looking at her. "Always the smart one."

Fern couldn't have been less interested in Jeremy or me. She sat us down in front of the television, while she and my mother sat on bar stools at the counter, drinking eggnog. I was used to this, to people wanting my mother to themselves. If, at a party, my mother left the room for a moment, everyone grew quiet. No one wanted to tell a story if she wasn't there to hear it.

"Do you ever miss Finland?" I heard Fern ask.

I strained my ears.

"I miss the solitude," my mother said.

"But you've always been so social."

"You have to be social when there are people around."

I made an effort to stare at the TV. I was afraid if I looked in my mother's direction, I might catch her gesturing toward Jeremy and me.

After an hour, I took Jeremy to the bathroom in case he needed to go. While sitting him down, I noticed all the wax that had accumulated in his left ear. I searched through Fern's medicine cabinet and Q-tipped out the buildup with such determination that Jeremy started to scream.

The outburst cut our visit short. My mother interpreted it as a sign Jeremy didn't like Fern's house, and I didn't disabuse her of this idea.

"I really like Fern," my mother said, once we were in the car. "I think she and I are going to be good friends again."

I knew better than to believe her fondness for Fern would last. The year before, she had said the same thing about Clara, and Irene, and Sandy, Christina, Sandy (a different one), Judy, and Patty. For at least a month, each of these women had my mother's full devotion. They were sent cards if they'd had a hard day, were given flowers if something had gone right at work. But she would then switch affections. She would simply stop taking their calls, and I'd be left answering the phone. My mother would stand in the hallway or beside me, instructing me to say she wasn't home. She signaled this with a sharp movement of her hand across her neck.

Dad apologized to people on her behalf when she'd said something uncouth; he collected her friends when she tossed them off. Maybe he knew it wouldn't be long before she shunned him as well. But Dad was a handsome man, and his friendships with the discarded women didn't sit well with their husbands. One of the women—Christina—gave me a note to pass along to him. I read it first. She had written, "If only you hadn't complimented my blouse in his presence ..."

4.

When we returned home from Fern's that afternoon, the neighbor's cat, Taft, was sitting on our porch. He was making his rounds earlier than usual. My mother searched in vain for milk. "Damn," she said.

In recent months, my mother had started talking to Taft. Every night after dinner, the cat would come to our porch and meow for my mother's attention and milk.

Dad was allergic to cats, to dogs, and my mother didn't hesitate to show her annoyance at his condition. I thought her visits with the cat would stop as the weather changed, but no. When fall approached, she would pull a blanket over her shoulders before heading out to the porch; come winter, she put on a parka.

She would sit outside for hours, talking to Taft. As it grew later, she'd stick her head inside the house and call up to me: "Did you finish your homework?" or "Did you brush your teeth?" I often lied in hopes she would come upstairs and reprimand me.

The second-floor bathroom was above the porch, and I would lean my head out, trying to hear what she was saying. I would catch a word or two, but usually she was whispering.

I complained to Dad one night. "She's talking to the damned cat again," I said. I was swearing to show I was mad; I was sure he would scold me.

"What do you say we kill it?" he said.

In the second before he started laughing, I saw that he was dead serious, his eyes dark as a gun.

5.

At five p.m. on December 16, my mother called me into her study. I waited until she said my name twice, so I didn't appear too eager.

She was sitting at her desk, a set of salt and pepper shakers before her. She had evidently poured out the contents of both onto her desk and was drawing patterns in the seasoning with her forefinger. I took a step back, wishing that this time I hadn't responded when summoned.

"Do you know why I named you Clarissa?" she asked, glancing in my direction. When she wanted it to appear she was looking me in the eye, she stared at my nose.

I nodded. "From the book."

I had been told that Dad had read *Mrs. Dalloway* to my mother when she was on bed rest.

"I named you after a book, yes," she said. "But not after *Mrs. Dalloway*. I named you after *Clarissa* by Samuel Richardson."

"Okay," I said.

"I didn't want to tell you until you were old enough because I was afraid you wouldn't understand. It's more complex than that. I named you after this Clarissa with the hope that you'd rewrite history."

"Wow," I said. I leaned against the wall for support.

"I've been meaning to have this talk with you. I'm glad we're having it now." She smiled at her desk.

I stared at her.

"If a man tries something on you, force yourself to pee. Use your legs—that's where your weight is. Gouge his eyes with your fingers. Punch his ears with your fists. Ruin his ability to see and hear. And then run."

When I opened my mouth, I made a point of speaking slowly, rationally, the way I addressed Jeremy when he was having a tantrum. "I'll remember that," I said.

Silence.

I looked over her shoulder at what she'd traced in the salt and pepper. I thought it would be a clue, a postscript to what she'd told me. In large capital letters, she had scrawled: BUY MILK.

6.

When Dad came home that evening, he looked after Jeremy while my mother and I went to the Poughkeepsie mall to do our Christmas shopping. After picking out a sweat suit for Dad and a telescope for Jeremy, we separated so we could buy each other gifts. We would meet up at the bakery at seven.

I went to the Body Shop to buy my mother bath oil. I inhaled the various scents. I asked the man behind the counter if I could get a sixteen-ounce bottle of vanilla bath oil. Gita always smelled of vanilla.

"Is it for you?" he asked.

"No, it's for my mom," I said. The pride in my voice surprised me.

"Well, this is a nice gift," he said. "You'll never see your mom after giving her this. She'll be spending all her time in the bath—reading, eating, sleeping even. You can get yourself into all sorts of trouble while she's not around." He winked.

I looked at my watch. It was a few minutes after seven. "Can you make it shower gel instead?" I asked.

"Sure, honey," he said. He took his time formulating the concoction, and then wrapped the bottle in pink cellophane and tied it with lavender ribbons. I knew I'd have to rewrap it when I got home; my mother thought Christmas presents should look like they were specifically for Christmas.

I got to the bakery late, at a quarter after.

The woman behind the counter noticed me. "Are you look-ing for a lady you were supposed to meet here?" she asked. She was wearing a red T-shirt silk-screened with two fried eggs, one over each breast.

I nodded.

"She said to tell you she got tired of waiting."

7.

I called Dad, and he and Jeremy came to pick me up. Dad said my mother wasn't at home when he left, and she hadn't called. "I'm sure she'll be there when we get back," he added.

At home, there was no sign of my mother's car. Nor was she in the house. Dad sat on the couch, holding a pillow over his face. The pillow was orange, with long, thin tassels, one of which was in his mouth. He put the pillow down in his lap. "Can you pass me the phone?" he said, though it wasn't far from him.

I brought it to him, and he dialed and then covered the mouthpiece. "It's the good Chinese restaurant. What do you want?"

8.

The next morning, when she hadn't returned, Dad called her California sisters. They hadn't heard from her. He called Fern, who hadn't, either. Then he called the police. "How long do you have to wait before reporting someone missing?" he asked.

Two detectives came to our house that afternoon. I described for them what my mother had been wearing at the mall: a black sweater covered in cat hair and a pair of brown suede pants that, at the knees and lap creases, had faded to the color of butter.

They asked if anything had been taken from the premises. "Everything's here," Dad said. "In order."

"Has she ever done anything like this before?"

Dad turned to me. "Clar, can you excuse us for a second? Maybe go check on Jeremy?"

I stared at him and then went upstairs to Jeremy's room. A friend of my mother's had given him a karaoke machine. Jeremy was watching the "Moon River" tape.

I crept back out to the landing above the stairway.

"She was married before," Dad was telling the detectives. "She left him without warning."

I had never heard of the first husband.

"Where does the ex-husband live?" one of the detectives asked.

"Finland. The northern part. He's a priest there. Or he was. A Sami man."

"A what?"

"Sorry. A native. Part of the native population. Like Eskimos."

"Any chance she went back to the priest? What was his name?"

"Eero. Eero Valkeapää." He spelled it for them. "And no, there's no chance. She was very unhappy with him. It's been more than a decade. Fifteen years since she saw him."

"Any reason for you to expect your wife might have been having an affair?"

"Out of the question," Dad said. "She wasn't ... how do I say this? Olivia wasn't a sexual person."

9.

I knew things Dad didn't.

I was eleven when my mother gave me her earrings. I was watching Jeremy one afternoon when he had a tantrum. He had carried anything with an electrical cord—the toaster, the blow dryer, the small TV from my parents' bedroom—into the center of the living room.

I looked all over the house for my mother. I found her out-side in the garden, kissing a man under the bird feeder. Like mistletoe, I thought. The man was Mr. Wells, the owner of the art-house theater in town. He was a drunk who attempted to disguise the stench of bourbon with an excessive application of Ben-Gay. I tried to sneak back into the house without them seeing me, but I'd locked the door.

"Here you go, baby," she said later that night. "The earrings are a tradition among the women in our family." She said her own mother had given her a pair of earrings when she was my age, and now she wanted to give them to me. "I can't wear them anyway," she said.

My mother had slits in her ears where her piercings once were. Years had caused the rips to split and separate, each one an inverted V, like the door to an unzipped tent.

"Here," she said. "Take them." With pinched fingers, she held the gold hoops out to me, as if holding dead mice by their tails.

Mr. Wells left town the following spring—most likely, his wife had found out about my mother—and moved to Texas. Shortly after he left, a package showed up at our door. The return address was in San Antonio.

Without opening it, my mother placed the package inside two of Jeremy's plastic bags—he kept his collection in the hall closet—tied the bags in a knot, and threw the bundle in the trash.

"Wrong address," she said to me.

Later, I ripped open the plastic bags. Inside was a miniature horse and a T-shirt that said DON'T MESS WITH TEXAS.

A scarecrow stood in the center of the small garden Dad had helped me plant. I dressed it in the DON'T MESS WITH TEXAS shirt. If my mother noticed, she never said a word.

10.

Two days after my mother vanished, I came home and her car was in the driveway. I ran into the house.

"The police found it parked at the Rhinecliff train station," Dad said.

I returned to the bakery in the mall and found the fried-egg lady. Now she was wearing an apron over a solid black shirt. I asked her if my mother had bought bread the evening of December 16. I wanted to know if she'd been planning on coming home for dinner, and then changed her mind.

The egg lady shrugged. "Sure," she said. "Sure, she bought bread."

11.

Two weeks after my mother disappeared, Virginia took me to see a psychic. She said she'd found one that specialized in my situation.

"You know, lost people," Virginia said.

The psychic had asked that I bring a photo. I'd selected

one of my mother standing in front of the movie theater. One day, as I was coming home from school, I saw her exiting the theater and I asked her to pose. In the picture, she was wearing white culottes and looked like she was forcing herself to be patient. "Why didn't anyone tell me how unbecoming those are on me?" she said when she saw the photo. She stared at me accusingly, and later donated the culottes to a charity clothing drive.

The psychic was sixty, maybe older. She held my fingers in hers and told me I was a sad, sad person, with a sad soul. "I can see it in your eyes. What lonely eyes." My hands were cold in her oily palms. I stared at her so long I thought I might start crying. I handed her the picture.

She held the photo up to her forehead and closed her eyes. Her lashes were beaded with blue mascara. "Someone has done harm to her," she said. "She's in a field and it was a bad man who did this to her."

"Did what?" I asked.

The psychic said she'd need more money to try to see the man, and the exact location of the field. She pushed a large jade bracelet up and down her thick, hairless forearm.

I had already given her the money I earned babysitting. I unclasped my coin purse. Red, ripped lining.

"Your earrings would do the trick," she said.

I touched my earlobes. I was wearing the earrings my mother had given me.

"They're from my mother," I stammered.

"Good," the psychic said. "It might help."

She reached for my ear. I leaned back in my chair and then jumped up. I found Virginia in the front of the parlor.

"Let's go," I said. "Let's run."

We sprinted down the street, hand in hand. We had never held hands before. We ran until we were out of breath, and fell laughing against the side of a grocery store. As Virginia laughed, she threw back her head, and her long hair brushed the rainbows on the pockets of her jeans. She had light eyes, good eyes—boys said they were bedroomy.

That night, I stared at myself in the mirror on the inside lid of an old jewelry box. I squinted my eyes, trying to make them look seductive, vague, distant.

12.

A month after my mother's disappearance, we hired Suzette. Suzette was an elderly Chinese woman who came in the afternoons to help us clean the house and look after Jeremy. Her own retarded son had died at the age of thirty. I couldn't piece together all the details: a Circle Line cruise around New York, a fascination with a seagull, a fall from the top deck.

Suzette thought she could understand Jeremy. "He said he missed you today," she told me one afternoon. I had just come home from school.

"Really?" I said. I'd never heard him speak. He could grunt when upset, but to my knowledge, he had never formed words.

I stood with my backpack still on, staring at Jeremy. He was sitting on the toilet, the door wide open. Suzette was trying to potty-train him. She paid a great deal of attention to his fecal matter: she'd serve him beef or large quantities of 7-Up if she thought he was having difficulty in either direction.

"Did you say you missed your sister when she was at school?" Suzette coaxed.

Jeremy said nothing.

"Did you miss me, Jeremy?" I said.

Nothing. I felt jealousy so intense I didn't know what it was. I wanted to slap Suzette. I stomped to my room, closed the door, and hoped my mother was dead in a field.

13.

Dad wrote letters to my mother. He wrote them by hand on long reams of old computer paper, the kind with the perforations on the sides. Some days, his letters, in clean all-caps, covered one sheet, other days, three. He never separated a page from the one before it. Instead, they remained fastened, top to bottom to top to bottom. When I first came upon the stack on the floor, I lifted up the top page only to find the next one pulled up beneath it. I stood on his desk chair and continued lifting, the letters forming an escalator, rising.

Initially, the letters gave me hope: Dad thought she was still alive. But then I remembered that he had written similar letters to his mother after she was dead.

I let the papers collapse, each page folding obediently, and stepped down from the chair.

14.

That March, I got lost while walking in the forest behind our house. I was plotting how I'd live out in the woods, surviving on berries, when Dad found me.

As we made our way back to the house, I tried to explain to him how I'd loved the thrill of thinking I was lost. He looked at me and nodded. "You're the way I was when I was young," he said, "when I traveled constantly and had no home."

In his twenties and thirties, Dad had lived in Haiti, the Andes, Canada. He'd written a book, published by a small academic press, about extracts from plants, which some Haitians used to induce trances. At thirty-eight, Dad moved to the Hudson River Valley to take care of his dying mother. To pay the bills, he became a landscape architect.

"Don't you miss it?" I said as he led me under trees, over a creek, back home.

"Miss what?"

"All the travel. It must be boring being with me and Jeremy all the time."

"Being with you guys ..." he said. "I'll never leave. You know that, don't you?"

I nodded. I had taken the suitcases from his closet and hidden them under my bed.

15.

On my sixteenth birthday, Virginia took me to a party in the next town. She dared me to lose my virginity that night. "I need to be able to talk to someone about what it's like," she said.

I felt too old to not have had sex. In every other way, I felt thirty. "How much do you dare me?" I said.

Virginia took a sip of beer instead of answering.

Two boys came into the kitchen. They asked if we wanted pot, and Virginia said sure, and I declined. I wanted to keep my brain fresh, alive, a note-taking classification machine.

"Oh my gosh," I said, looking at one of their T-shirts. "That's my dad." At home, we had boxes of these T-shirts my father gave out to his clients. The boy looked down at his shirt. "Your father's Richard of Richard's Landscape?"

I nodded.

The two boys looked at each other and laughed. I had no idea what was funny, but I felt exiled by their laughter, so I laughed, too. The boy in my father's shirt turned around, and I understood the joke. On the back, at the end of the list of services provided—SOD, STONE WALLS, TREE AND STUMP REMOVAL—it said BUSH TRIMMING.

I took a sip of my beer, and then another, longer one. To explain the tears in the corners of my eyes, I made an exaggerated pretense of choking on the beer, on the hilarity of it all.

It was someone's idea that we go to the park. Christian, the boy wearing my father's T-shirt, was leading me by the elbow.

As we approached the playground, my feet sank, and I collapsed in the sand by the swings. The voices of the others surrounded us, sounding alternately loud and absent, like a stereo with only one speaker working.

Christian led me to the small merry-go-round. I sat down, and he spun me. I lay on my back and saw the obsidian sky above and heard the quacks of ducks in the distance. Where were the others? Christian came and lay down next to me, and the spinning slowed slightly as my heartbeat quickened. He put his hands on either side of my face and kissed me. His fingers smelled of metal, of other people's fingers.

I was wearing a vintage dress with butterflies, and he searched for the zipper. "It's on the side," I murmured. But by this time, he'd given up. He lifted up the skirt, and the breeze against my thighs felt almost wet. My hands were flat against the floor of the merry-go-round. Christian grabbed my left hand and put it on his crotch. He'd unzipped his pants. We were slowing down now, slow slow slow. I tried to pull my hand off, but he held it there, on him. I used the fingers of my free hand to poke him in the eye, the way my mother had taught me. Then I stuck my foot out and stopped the spinning; I pushed him off me and jumped.

As I ran through the park, I heard Christian calling after me. "Hey, crazy girl. You're fucking insane." I almost fell into the pond. Sleeping ducks awakened and scattered—the sound of a hundred decks of cards shuffled at once.

The next day, I walked by the psychic's storefront window,

with my seductive bedroom eyes. I hoped she would see me and know she'd gotten me wrong. *Try to recognize me now.*

16.

I went looking for my mother once, the summer before my senior year of high school. I convinced Virginia to drive to Texas with me.

"Texas?" she said.

"Yeah," I said. "I think that's where my mom lives now."

Virginia looked at me, head tilted. "Okay," she said, and picked something from between her small teeth.

I had convinced myself that my mother had gone to join Mr. Wells. I had kept the envelope in which the DON'T MESS WITH TEXAS shirt had been sent. The return address was in San Antonio.

Virginia and I saved up from our summer jobs, and at the end of August, we packed her brother's Camaro. We brought a tent, sleeping bags, a cooler, old yearbooks, and a road map I'd gotten from AAA. Our route was highlighted in orange.

Every time we crossed a state border, we gave each other a compliment. "I like that you're a loyal friend, a constant friend," I told Virginia when we entered Oklahoma.

"I like that you think the best of me," she said in return.

When we got to San Antonio, the sky was mustard-colored and heavy with impending rain. We bought baseball hats and big, dark sunglasses and parked across the street from the address I had for Mr. Wells. We sat there for two days, sipping Diet Cokes and watching. Virginia had her disposable camera ready, though I wasn't sure what she was going to document. If we saw my mother entering or leaving the house, I didn't need it on film.

On the third day, Virginia suggested we knock on the door. "We don't have all the time in the world," she said. "School starts next week."

We rang the doorbell. We heard furniture shifting inside.

"Jesus," I said. "He's home."

The door opened. "Can I help you?" said a young man.

"Do you live here?" Virginia asked.

"Yes."

"Alone?"

He nodded. He had curly black hair and dry lips, and he was all the better-looking for not being Mr. Wells.

"Do you know a Mr. Wells?" I said.

"Yeah, he's my landlord."

He asked us to excuse him—he had the flu. He'd been in bed for days. *How sad,* I thought, *no one came to take care of you. We were watching, and no one came.*

He gave us Tim Wells's address, and that evening, we went to his house, in a different, less appealing part of town. Virginia rang the doorbell while I stood at the bottom of the steps. A redheaded woman answered the door, said she was Mr. Wells's wife. He was at a meeting but would be home at nine. "Can I help you girls?" she asked. She was the kind of woman who asked questions with her hands on her hips.

"That's okay," Virginia said.

We waited on the neighbors' steps. By ten, he still hadn't shown up. "Maybe his wife told him to come in the back door," Virginia offered. "What kind of meeting would he be at this late?"

"He used to drink," I said.

"Oh, right."

At ten thirty, we saw Mr. Wells get out of a dented Datsun. His hair was thinner now; he wore a striped jacket over a striped shirt. I was outraged he had made us wait so long. I intercepted him before he made it to the stairs of his house.

"Where were you?" I said. I felt emboldened by the days of waiting. "You were supposed to be home at nine. Were you at your girlfriend's house?"

He raised his briefcase like he was going to use it to hit me. Then he placed it down on the ground. It toppled over. "Who are you?"

"You don't remember?"

"No," he said, shaking his head. "What's going on?"

I asked him if he knew where my mom was.

"Your mom?"

"Olivia," Virginia interjected.

"Jesus Christ. Is that what this is about? I haven't seen that crazy lady for three or four years."

"Don't call her crazy," I said.

"You swear you haven't seen her?" Virginia said.

"Boy Scout's honor," Mr. Wells said, and started laughing. I almost spat at him.

Virginia and I looked at each other, not knowing whether to continue pressing him for details, for proof, but his laughter defeated us.

We headed back to New York that night. Going in this direction, we hardly said a word.

17.

The year my mother disappeared, I began following missing persons cases. It had surprised me that when families found the bodies of their loved ones, they told news reporters they finally felt a sense of closure, of relief. But after Texas, I began to see how this could be true. If someone gave me a pile of bones and said they were my mother's, I decided I would cry for a day and move on.

Other girls in my class dated and went to school dances and proms, but I wasn't interested. When I started college, I lied and told people I was in a long-distance relationship. I almost began to believe I was involved with someone. He lived in San Antonio, I told my new friends, and when I pictured him, he was the young man with curly black hair who lived in the house where my mother did not.

18.

On the fourth anniversary of my mother's departure, Dad and I had a funeral for her, behind my vegetable garden. We were the only ones invited, the only attendees. We had no proof she was dead, but we needed to feel that she was. We filled a soup terrine she had loved—a wedding present—with some of her favorite possessions: the earrings she'd given me, a golf ball she had found in the woods (she thought it brought her luck), a red silk blouse with three buttons missing, and a matchbook collection she'd started when she'd visited Lisbon in her twenties.

"So long," I said. I was on my knees, patting snow over the soup terrine, like I was firming the foundation for a snowman. "Fare thee well."

Family Portrait Above Altar

1.

I woke at six-thirty and checked the hotel bathroom. I was surprised to see Kari was still on the floor, on his stomach. His feet were sticking out beneath the sheet, his heels dry and deeply cracked.

I turned on the faucet, muffling it with a hand towel, which I used to rinse off. It was what my mother used to call a whore's bath, and this seemed appropriate. After dressing in the same clothes I'd worn the night before, I slowly zipped my suitcase, joining only a few teeth at a time in an attempt to stay quiet. Kari's pants, shirt, and sad sweater were nested together on the floor. I opened the door to the room gently and closed it silently. There was only the click as it locked behind me.

I picked up my passport at reception. The woman at the front desk didn't ask how my stay was, and for this I was thankful. Outside, snow fell like baby powder. I pulled my suitcase behind me and felt comforted by the steady sound of its one good wheel bumping over cobblestones.

The train station was three blocks away. A cab stopped—I thought, for me, a likely suspect with the suitcase. But no: a man and a woman in their early twenties tumbled out of the backseat, holding beer bottles. They left their bottles on the street, propping them carefully upright, and disappeared into a doorway. Seconds after they closed the door behind them, one beer bottle fell over with a clamor. It rolled past four parked cars, gathered speed, and continued until it reached the bottom of the hill, where it hit a curb and shattered.

As I passed in front of a department store, the lights in the window snapped on, and the sound of "Silent Night" blared through a speaker. Startled, I almost twisted my ankle. In slow motion, and accompanied by a ticking sound, the mannequins in the window rotated left and right. A dog's tail wagged. A small boy in a striped sweater extended a present toward me, then retracted it. The mouths of women in traditional dress dropped open. I quickened my pace.

At the train station, I asked a man behind the ticket counter how to get to Inari. There were no direct trains, he said. I would have to take a twelve-hour train ride to Rovanemi, and from Rovanemi I'd take a bus to Ivalo, and from Ivalo I'd take another bus to Inari. It would be a twenty-one-hour trip. I unsuccessfully searched my map for the towns he was mentioning. The man redirected my gaze. I hadn't been looking far enough north.

I booked a sleeper, sat on a bench, and waited to depart for the town where, according to the Finnish phone book, Eero Valkeapää, my real father, still lived. A pigeon flew into the train station and sat at my feet. I kicked it with my boot. Watching it scurry, stumble, and fly away was more satisfying than anything I'd done in weeks.

2.

The train was called The Santa Claus Express. I boarded and searched for my sleeper. As I approached my compartment, two men smoking cigarettes ducked inside. I had assumed I would be in a smokeless compartment, alone—not with two men. I almost wept. I hadn't realized how tired I was, how unable I felt to remedy a mistake.

I stood outside the door to my compartment, and the men stood inside. I showed them my ticket. The men, it turned out, had stepped inside to let me pass. They shuffled out and nodded, leaving behind a plume of unfiltered smoke. My stomach curled—it was empty and I was hungover. I had been so angry at those men, and now I was angry that I had been angry.

Each room in second class had three berths. Mine was the middle one. I turned the pillow so I could look out the window, and placed my backpack at my feet. I took off my jacket and crawled under the comforter. Clean and white and soft.

As the train left the station, I pressed my forehead to the cold window. We started out slow, passing houses the color of Viking ships in children's books—utterly confident blues, reds, yellows. Ladders led to the rooftops, to ease the shoveling off of snow. Parted curtains in the windows revealed the same scene: seven lighted white candles, all balanced on an upside-down V.

The farther north we traveled, the darker it grew. By three o'clock, it was already night.

3.

We arrived in Rovanemi after midnight. My bus wouldn't be leaving until six a.m. I sat in a coffee shop adjacent to the train station, and when that closed, I lay on a bench inside the waiting area. I slept with my purse held close to me, like an infant. On a nearby bench, a woman slept with her baby held close to her, like a purse.

The bus, when it came, was double-deckered. I sat on the top level, toward the back, away from the schoolboys listening to unquiet headphones. I removed my boots, but my feet were so cold on the footrest I had to sit on them. The bus stopped at every town to pick up mail, drop off packages. On the side of the roads, children walked to school, their flashlights casting yellow circles on the snow.

On the bus from Rovanemi to Ivalo, I finally grew impatient with travel. Until then, I'd liked that the trip was taking so long: I had time to plan what I would say to Eero Valkeapää. But on this, the second-to-last leg, I didn't want to think, didn't want to read any of the books I had brought. Restless, I flipped through the in-flight magazine from my SAS flight from Brussels to Helsinki. Hans Blix was on the cover, pictured relaxing in a black leather chair. I read the article about him. He was Scandinavian—that I knew. But I hadn't known he had two sons, a wife. I stared at his picture for a long, long time. I bet Hans Blix was a damn good father.

4.

A woman who looked like my dentist was sitting two rows ahead of me. She got off the bus at the cemetery, leaving behind her scarf, gray and thick. I picked it up and wrapped it around my neck. It smelled clean, like snow.

When we approached Inari, the bus driver signaled it was my stop. "Hello, English," he called out.

"Hotel?" I asked.

With a gloved finger, he pointed down the road.

I dragged my suitcase behind me, unsure whether its wheels were rolling on the ice or sliding. The sun never rose, but at ten thirty, the sky looked like a dark blue parachute concealing a flame.

I turned down a narrow road toward a colony of cabins and moved faster, feeling colder at the prospect of imminent warmth. I rang the bell of the main house, waited, and then turned the knob. The door opened a crack: a woman with her shirt unbuttoned was nursing a baby. I averted my eyes from her breasts. Inside the entranceway stood several pairs of boots—those of a woman, a man, at least two children, and a baby, all in a row. A family of footwear.

The woman said something in Finnish. I stared at her.

"How many night?" she said in English.

I wasn't sure how much time Eero Valkeapää and I would need together. "One week?" I asked, still looking at the boots.

5.

The woman put on a coat and, carrying the baby, escorted me to a cottage. It had one bunk bed, two single beds, a kitchenette, a table, and a bathroom. The extra beds made me feel small, alone in a dollhouse.

I asked where the church was.

"Which kind?" she said.

"Sami."

It was down the road, right before the center of town. As she was leaving, she placed the key in my palm, as if it was a communion wafer, and pressed lightly.

I sat in front of the heater and warmed my feet until my damp socks smelled of burned wool. I pulled on another sweater, unhooked a flashlight from the cottage's coat rack, and headed out. It was significantly easier to walk without the suitcase—my body felt lighter, sleeker, free. I came upon the start of a town, and to the side of the road, a white wooden church. Fifteen cars were parked in the lot. I looked at my watch: twenty minutes past noon. Sunday.

I approached the brown doors of the church and stared at the gold handles. I hadn't expected it to be so easy. Everything had gone so slowly until now.

No one turned as I entered the church. I sat toward the back, across the aisle from a little girl. The church wasn't crowded, but everyone was spread out—two or four people per pew. The congregation consisted of grandparents with their grandchildren; the generation in between was missing.

The older women wore black dresses, embroidered with red and green; the men, black tunics, similarly trimmed. The grandchildren, in their early teens, were dressed for snowboarding.

I couldn't put it off any longer: I forced myself to look in the direction of the priest.

I knew it without thinking. My father.

He stood behind a pulpit, wearing a white robe with a green sash. His eyes were dark, like mine, set deep in his face. His hair was the white of doves' feathers, but his face was youthful, handsome though gaunt. His white robe looked large on his body, as though he had recently lost weight. Was he sick? *Not another funeral. Not now, after finding him at last.*

He gestured while he spoke: he made fists and open-handed gestures; he stared up at the ceiling and then looked compassionately out toward his congregation. Could he see me? Did he know? I was afraid I might stand. Or jump. In my boots, my toes tingled as they defrosted. When he extended his hands outward, I reached mine forward and touched the pew in front of me.

There was the sound of creaking, of furniture shifting. The congregation was kneeling to pray. I leaned forward, my knees hitting the hard floor. Everyone around me had closed their eyes, but I watched my father through my lashes. I watched him without blinking, until my eyes started to tear. I could see why he would make a good priest: his voice was deep and calming and caring, the voice of a contented man. I felt proud of him. I felt proud of myself. *You are who I come from. I am more like this man than my mother. I am you, my father.*

Above the altar hung not a cross, not Jesus, but a portrait of a family—parents, son, daughter, all in traditional clothing. The same outfits worn by the older members of the congregation. In this church, you gave thanks to family.

My father began setting the communion table. He took more steps than seemed necessary to bring each object to its proper place. I was unsure whether or not to take communion. I was afraid of being that close to him, of his looking me in the eye as he pressed the wafer into the palm of my hand. *Like a key.* It would be unfortunate if he recognized me. Or worse if he did not.

The first row rose for communion. Trying not to call attention to my departure, I left through the same doors of the church through which I had entered.

6.

Outside, the sky was streaked chartreuse, white-blue, salmon— colors from a freezer opened in a dark room.

I went in search of food. I walked toward the small town on the snowy road—there was no sidewalk—and past the tourist information center, now closed. The posters in the window advertised a trip to Santa Land, a snowmobiling excursion, a vacation in Thailand. A large souvenir shop sold handmade jewelry and dolls wearing traditional black dresses. SAMI HANDI-

CRAFTS, said the sign. Hundreds of reindeer horns and stuffed animals, all huskies, on display in the window. They had probably been there for years, and would remain unsold.

I was born here, I thought, and looked around with pride. *I was born here.* The town was bleak, small, struggling.

I entered a restaurant by the lake, now frozen. I took a seat but couldn't understand the menu. A waitress came to take my order, and I requested what I hoped was a sandwich.

The wall by my table was lined with gambling machines and old black-and-white photos of men I assumed were locals. Some were wearing Sami outfits; most were wearing hats. None were my father. In the corner, boys who looked no more than twelve were shooting pool. Dire Straits played on the jukebox, and Angela Lansbury was solving a murder on the TV.

Three o'clock. It was possible Eero Valkeapää would be home by now, and if not, I could go back to the church. Everyone else would have left, returned home to their families, to their Sundays. The restaurant was loud, and even if I located a phone, I didn't want to call from there. I paid the waitress and walked outside.

Near a small supermarket stood a phone booth with a glass door, a Superman phone booth. I took out the number I'd copied from the phone book and called my father.

7.

A man answered the phone.

"Eero?" I asked. I wasn't sure if I was pronouncing it correctly. I didn't know how to say my own father's name.

The man indicated that he was Eero, and then said something else.

"Do you speak English?" I asked. Dumb question. My mother didn't speak Finnish.

"Yes," he said.

"It's Clarissa."

"Clarissa?" he said.

"Yes."

There was a long pause.

"Olivia's daughter?" he asked.

"Yes," I said. *And your daughter, too.*

"Where are you calling from? California?"

It struck me that he had no idea where my mother went when she left, just as Richard hadn't had a clue. "I'm ... I'm here in Inari."

"Here!"

"Yeah, yes, here. In town."

"Your mother ... she has died?" he asked.

Who Sleeps Where in the *Lavu*

1.

Eero Valkeapää and I agreed to meet in front of the restaurant at five p.m. I walked along the main road through town, venturing farther than I'd gone before—over the bridge, with its view of snowmobile tracks on the lake, and toward the Sami museum. When the cold had come into my coat, I returned to the restaurant and, along with the old men, watched an episode of a home-improvement show devoted to renovating saunas.

At ten to five, I moved outside. I wiped the snow from a bench, and, before sitting, pulled my jacket down to cover the seat of my pants. A bus stopped in front of me, and I sat up straight, but no one got off; the bus driver had opened the door on my account. The door closed, and the bus continued down the road.

Across the street, a woman with a cane shuffled by and, two minutes later, passed again. She was out exercising. I alone seemed affected by the cold.

As I was checking my watch, I heard a man's voice. I looked up, and it was my father.

"Olivia's daughter?" he said.

"Yes."

"Eero," he said. It rhymed with *hero*. I almost laughed.

"Clarissa," I said. I stood and extended my hand. His gloved palm enveloped three of my fingers, the way adults hold the hands of small children.

"The car is this way," he said. "I think we go back to the house and talk?"

He didn't move until I took a step in the direction he'd pointed. I had to remind myself to walk, to breathe. I felt like I was on a first date with someone I had loved from afar.

"My English is a little rusted. You excuse me?" he said. "You are the woman who comes into church today."

"Yes." We were both looking at the ground, making sure we didn't slip. The snow beneath my feet sparkled like sunlit cement.

He opened the car door for me and got in on his side. When he turned on the engine, the radio came on so loud I jumped in my seat. Eero made no indication that he was going to turn down the volume, so I did.

"Where do you live in America?" he asked.

"New York."

"Oh, New York!" he said.

I asked if he had ever been there.

"No," he said. "I go to Santa Fe once, and to California?"

"With my mother?"

"No. When I was looking for her?" He gave a sideways glance in my direction. I decided I'd ask about that later. I had to pace things.

"How long have you lived here?"

"I am born here?" he said. Kari spoke in accusations, Eero in questions.

We slowed as we turned onto a street lined with one-story A-frame houses. "This is our street," he said. All the houses but one had a single strand of white Christmas lights bordering a garage door, or running along a roof.

"Everyone is very upset with that house," Eero said, gesturing at a house with blue lights outlining the front door. "Those people really took it too far."

2.

He opened the door, and two dogs rushed to greet me. "Pia and Emma," he announced.

"Are they huskies?" I said, tentatively petting Pia.

"Yes, for hunting elk," he said.

He took off his boots, and I took off mine. I placed them underneath a bench in the hallway, next to a pair of clogs, the heels of which were drastically worn down. *The woman who replaced my mother.* Based on the heels, I decided she had a funny walk.

"Is your wife home?" I asked.

"No, she directs the choir at the church. She works with them to get ready the Christmas service," he said.

"She has a beautiful voice," he said, and I said, "Oh, that's too bad," at the same time.

It was already apparent to me what a good home my mother would have had here, what a good husband Eero would have made.

"Would you like coffee?" Eero offered. Now in proximity, and in the light, I could study him. He had two skin tags on his forehead. They were so narrow at their point of attachment, they could have been cut off with a pair of small scissors.

I said I'd have coffee if he was having some, and followed him into the kitchen. I had assumed my father would be short, that his lack of height would explain mine, but Eero was tall, especially for a Sami. Every detail seemed extraordinary. His slow walk, his mended socks, the loop he had missed when threading his belt around his waist.

Eero pulled out a chair for me. "Welcome," he said.

"Thank you." Dad had had good manners, but he had never pulled out my chair.

I looked around. *This could have been the house I grew up in.* The kitchen table matched the wood throughout the house. It was blond, the kind that looked fitting in a summer cabin but seemed too light, too unsturdy for winter. The refrigerator was smaller than American refrigerators, with paneling that matched the wood of the floor. The kitchen led into what looked like a study, filled with dark furniture, its leather the color of men's dress shoes. *Where would my room have been?*

Eero moved around the kitchen the way he had when he was setting up the communion table at his church: he was judicious, and took more steps than seemed necessary. He opened a cupboard and returned to the table with a basket lined with a napkin and filled with crisp Wasa bread. Then he went to the refrigerator and came back with butter. Next, he opened the freezer, took out something wrapped in plastic, sliced it up, and approached the table with what looked like brown licorice. "Reindeer meat," he said, offering me a plate. He sat down across from me.

I picked up a slender slice of reindeer meat and took a small bite. It was salty, the texture like beef jerky. "Delicious," I said. I exaggerated a smile.

"How is your mother?" Eero said suddenly. He had buttered a piece of Wasa bread, but it lay resting on his plate.

"I don't know," I said. "She took off when I was fourteen."

"Took off?" he said.

"Left. She left me and Richard, her husband"—I looked to see if he knew, but his startled expression showed that he hadn't known she'd remarried—"and my brother, and never came back. This was in New York."

"Does she pack anything?"

"No." I was used to this line of questioning. Everyone thought they were a detective. "Did you call the police?" they'd say. "Did you look for a note?"

"I'm sorry for you," Eero said.

I studied his face. I was unaccustomed to sympathy without judgment, sympathy without condescension. I nodded at Eero. He knew how she did it. He knew it was not a matter of interrogating past lovers or combing a lake.

3.

There was still plenty of bread on the table, but Eero brought out more. "When she leave me she doesn't say anything, either," he said, arranging the new bread.

He paused. I could hear a neighbor calling out for their dog or perhaps their child.

"It is not so easy to be the wife of priest, to be the wife of Sami priest, in a town like this," he said. He gestured around the room, as though indicating that the kitchen was the town, or the town was the kitchen. "Yes," he said, agreeing with himself. "It is quite difficult."

"Did my mother pray?"

"Of course," Eero said. "Doesn't she raise you with religion?"

"No," I said. "I never saw her pray, either," I added. I couldn't picture her with her eyes closed.

"Your mother has no patience for this life here," Eero said. "She has her studies and her project."

"The indigenous peoples thing," I said, more to myself than to him.

"Indigenous," he repeated. "I think that's why daily life here disappoints her. Yes, she is disappointed."

He tapped the fingers of his left hand on the back of his right.

"She comes here thinking this place will give her wisdom into the Sami, that she helps with their cause. But people here are not aware of this cause of the Sami. We do not think of it that way back then—things are different now. I think for her research, and for the idea she has in her head, this is disappointing for her."

"It was disappointing for her," I said, trying to get him to use the past tense. Speaking about her in the present made me uncomfortable.

"I never forget how I meet her. I come back here from seminary school and she comes to church one day. I am filling in for the last pastor, who is sick. He dies that year, and I take his place. After she comes to church service, she asks me why I don't do all of the service in Sami. I explain that not everyone here speaks Sami, that I want to speak Finnish so more people understand. She is very upset about this. To her it isn't right. It isn't ..."

"It wasn't authentic?"

"Yes, authentic. It isn't the authentic experience she is looking for. This is why she is so interested in the Alta Dam."

"The dam?"

"In Finnmark?"

I shook my head.

"You don't know about the dam?" Eero looked at me quizzically. It was a face I myself often made.

"No," I said. I wanted him to hug me. It seemed ridiculous that after so long, I would have to sit across the table from him, my father. I wanted to leap into him.

I leaned closer to the table; he leaned back in his chair.

4.

In the seventies, he said, the Norwegian government announced plans to build a dam in the north of Norway, in Finnmark, the area where Norwegian and Finnish Lapland came together. The dam would be near the city of Alta, and would, the government claimed, generate not only electricity for southern Norway but hundreds of jobs for the local Sami. There was one hitch: the dam would redirect the flow of the river, and a historic Sami town called Masi would be flooded. Masi had a population of two hundred Sami.

My mother was one of the early protesters in the mid-1970s, and one of the only non-Sami involved. In 1980, when the building of the dam commenced, a large number of Sami chained themselves to each other to create a human roadblock to prevent workers from getting to the construction site. One man, who was trying to use explosives to bring down a bridge that led to the dam, blew off his arm.

In a sense, Eero explained, the Alta Dam protests were extremely important for the Sami. Before the protests, Sami villages hadn't felt connected to one another, but they banded together to oppose the construction of the dam.

"So what happened?" I asked. "Was the dam built?"

Ultimately, Eero said, the dam was built, on a smaller scale, and the town of Masi was saved.

"So my mother must have been happy," I said.

"Happy?" Eero said. "No, not this word for her. She leaves

me before the construction of the dam begins. She is very ...
disturbed after what happens in Masi."

"With the protests?"

"Yes, the protests," he said, "but also ..." He paused. Then
he moved his coffee cup to the side, as though it was its placement between us that was hindering conversation. "Do you not
know, my child? Masi is where you are conceived."

This seemed like inappropriate information for a priest
to be delivering. Or for a father. But he stated it in a factual
manner. It was possible that in Sami culture, greater impor-
tance was given to the place of conception.

There was a long silence, during which Eero observed me
sharply. Perhaps he knew he had surprised me with his disclo-
sure. And why was I so stunned by what he was trying to say?
He was corroborating what I'd suspected and at some level,
knew to be true: that my birth was not a joyous event for my
mother.

The sound of the phone startled me. On the third ring, as
though just hearing it for the first time, Eero stepped into the
hallway—a strange place for a phone—to answer it.

5.

Eero sat on a bench as he talked. I could see his feet. He
adjusted his socks so they were snug around his toes. I heard
him say "Olivia" and "Clarissa" and "America."

He came back to the table. "My wife, Kirsi," he said. "She is home in an hour."

"Did your wife know my mother?" I asked.

"Yes," he said.

Below my knees, my pants were carpeted with white dog hair. I picked off a few strands.

"Kirsi and your mother are not friends. They don't like the other."

Many people didn't like my mother. But Kirsi had no right to judge her. *Well, I don't like Kirsi*, I wanted to say.

"Kirsi's husband, Johan, he passes away suddenly—he has a heart attack. After they are married. I perform the funeral service," he said. "*Perform* is the right word?"

I nodded, and then second-guessed myself. "That or *presided over*."

"I *presided* the funeral service?"

"*Performed* is fine," I said, changing my mind.

"Kirsi needs much support after Johan's death, and she comes here every afternoon for coffee. I was typically not here—we have to be at the church. But it is your mother's duty to be here."

"Duty?"

"A priest's wife is to have coffee and keep food for people who visit. She has to be at the house between eight in the morning until four in the evening every day. She is here in case someone visit and need to talk. A widow. Or someone who lose a child. Anyone. She offers them food and warmth and care. She prays for them. It is her duty."

I stared at him.

"I know you being American think it's sexism and unfeminism, but that's her job." He sighed deeply.

"I have a long talk with her before we marry—in the church here in Inari. I tell her the expectations. And she is accepting of it. She says she is willing."

It was strange if not impossible to picture my mother marrying in a church in Finland. She and Dad were married in a friend's living room in Rhinebeck. I had seen a picture—my mother in a light blue dress and Dad in a suit, with a salmon-colored tie and tight shoes. He mentioned the discomfort of the shoes when he was looking at the photo, as if they were responsible for what happened to their marriage.

"She knows the life that is going to be hers," Eero continued. "And she cannot do this. She wants to travel. She wants her life to be bigger." He gestured broadly, as if conjuring great clouds. "This is why she goes to the protest in Masi."

I tried to think of what she was missing in her life in Rhinebeck. What had driven her away the second time?

"Are you married?" Eero asked.

"Engaged," I said, and suddenly felt sick over my behavior in Helsinki. I was still engaged, and while Pankaj had kept what he knew about my life a secret, he had not done what I had done.

"So I'm sure that you and your soon husband—what is his name?"

"Pankaj."

"You have many discussions about the future."

"Of course," I said, and then wondered if this were true.

"So like you and ..."

"Pankaj," I repeated.

"Pankaj. Like you, we talk over everything. I tell her I have my calling when I am twenty-three and she knows how much I work since then. I go to divinity school in Helsinki and then come back up here to be with my people."

"You mean your town, or the Sami?"

"The Sami. And my town. Almost everyone in this town is Sami."

Someone passed in front of the house, and the dogs barked like seals.

"When are you marrying?" he asked.

"We haven't set a date yet," I said.

Eero nodded, and I was sure that he knew.

6.

I excused myself to go to the bathroom. The room had a violet color scheme—violet towels, violet shower curtain, green-and-violet floor mat.

Inside the medicine cabinet were five frosted glass shelves, three of which were filled with remedies for back pain. Some had English translations on the back of the bottle; others had drawings of a spine on fire.

I opened the drawers beneath the sink, searching. I doubted I would discover anything—it had been so long ago—but I wanted to find something my mother had left behind. Something I would recognize. Toothpaste. At home, she had tubes of Colgate, Aim, Tom's of Maine. It bored her to go to sleep with the same taste in her mouth every night.

But here, there was nothing.

I was furious at Kirsi's ex-husband for dying. Kirsi wasn't my stepmother, nor had she robbed my mother of a husband, but she had made my mother's presence here invisible. Richard had done the same thing when my mother left home. Aside from her card catalog and a few of her books, Richard had stored everything in a rented unit in Poughkeepsie. When she hadn't returned, he stopped paying the bills; her belongings were lost. And now, no trace of her was to be found here, either. She was gone from every corner of the world, every storage unit and bathroom.

The dogs were waiting for me when I got out of the bathroom, and they followed me to my seat. Eero had cleared the table, leaving the coffee. I tried not to think about how many trips it had taken him to transport everything back to the cupboards, the refrigerator, the sink. He was now in the adjoining room, on his knees, opening and closing drawers. High drawers meant valuable things. Low drawers meant the past.

"Here are some pictures of her," he said, returning to the table with a large envelope. "You can keep them."

Instead of handing the envelope to me, he placed it on the table. It was as if he didn't want to be responsible for what I might find, for forcing the photos into my life.

I picked up the envelope. "Thank you."

"You are welcome," he said. "I am thinking I take you back to where you stay. Tomorrow, you can come here again, if you like. I go to Ivalo in morning, but I am back in afternoon. You can meet Kirsi."

I nodded. I was thirsty from the reindeer meat, so, I helped myself to a glass of water, drank it all, and then put on my jacket and followed him out to the Volvo. We passed two cars on the road, one of which winked its lights at Eero. He honked in return.

"Maybe you see the fires when you are here," Eero said.

"The fires?"

"The fires," he said, pointing to the sky. "The north lights."

"I hope so," I said.

"We believe they are our ancestors."

"Oh." I didn't know what else to say.

We turned in to the complex of cabins where I was staying.

"It was lovely meeting you, finally," I said. And then, impulsively, I leaned into him and hugged him. He stiffened with surprise. Perhaps he thought my mother would have spoken ill of him, when the truth was much sadder: she had never spoken of him at all.

I took the photos in my hand and opened the car door. I turned and leaned down before closing it. "See you tomorrow," I said.

"Sleep well, my child," he said.

As his headlights faded, I walked back to my cabin, repeating his words. *My child, my child, my child.*

7.

In my cabin, I sat at the table and opened the envelope. It was fastened with a black string around a red wheel. The wheel showed no sign of age. Eero had not opened this envelope often.

There were five photos, fewer than I expected. The top one was facedown. My first thought upon turning it over was that Eero had given me the wrong file. The woman looked nothing like the mother I had known.

But a second look revealed that it was her, younger and less restless—a woman who looked straight into the camera and whose eyes squinted with a smile. In another photo, her front teeth were biting down on her lower lip, as though to keep her from laughing aloud. From her ears hung the gold hoop earrings she had given me.

She looked the same in all the photos—which is to say, she looked different. Three pictures appeared to have been taken inside Eero's house. The other two on his porch, in the summer. In one, in color, she was petting a dog. A husky. Her brow was unfurrowed, and she was looking out into the distance, as though a bird or a sound had caught her attention in the moment before the click.

She seemed more comfortable being observed, being admired, than the mother who raised me. I slid the photos back into the envelope and wound the string around the red wheel so many times that the string's tail was no longer visible. Seeing the pictures was like spotting a former teacher swimming at a pool, or seeing a cop barking directions from the back of a taxi. Beyond the realm of Richard, Jeremy, and me, my mother was acting out of character; she was undamaged and blithe.

8.

I slept fitfully. When I woke, my mind felt blanketed, and I stayed in bed for much of the morning, calculating how few hours I had slept in the past week. Hunger finally roused me, and I dressed and walked to town. Inside the store that sold reindeer horns, I ate an overly sweet pastry and drank a cup of pale tea.

At the tourist information center, I bought a map and postcards of the town. I didn't plan on sending them to anyone, but I wanted to have proof that this place existed.

For two euros, said a sign, I could check my e-mail on the tourist center's computer. I paid. In my inbox were nine e-mails from Pankaj, two from Virginia, eight from various coworkers, and two from a film company in Hong Kong, a sister company to Soutitre. I didn't open any of the messages from Pankaj, or Virginia, or any of my coworkers. Instead, I read the e-mails from Hong Kong, as well as those from people whom I hadn't been in touch with recently, people who were unlikely to have heard about Dad's death or my sudden departure. I told three people I was writing from Bulgaria. When I tired of that, I said I was in Sydney, that the Opera House was atrocious but the steak was good. I told the Hong Kong company I would consider their job offer. It seemed true enough—there was nothing I wasn't contemplating.

In the late afternoon, when I surmised my father would be home from his trip to Ivalo, I walked by his house. In some respects, it wasn't much different from our house in Rhinebeck—both had three steps leading up to the front door, a small porch, a neatly stacked supply of firewood.

I rang the doorbell. Did people here ring doorbells? It seemed like a town where you would knock. A woman in her late fifties opened the door. She said something in Finnish.

"Hi," I said. "I'm Clarissa."

She stared at my mouth. Was she reading my lips? Did they resemble Eero's? Her eyes were dense black buttons, her hair the shade of lint. She invited me in.

I had been picturing Kirsi as the age my mother had been when she left. But Kirsi was older. She was large, ungainly, wearing a dress over corduroy pants.

Kirsi offered me coffee, and I settled for tea. She directed me toward the living room, which I hadn't seen the night before. While she was in the kitchen, I looked around the room. A large animal horn—a musical instrument of some kind—hung on the wall. I stroked its edges with my fingers. It had the texture of a tooth. In the corner stood a simple piano. A well-worn music book had been left open on the stand, and the seat bench was pulled out, as though the player had just gotten up.

Kirsi entered the living room with a tray. She poured me a cup of tea, and I thanked her. I tried to avoid looking at her cold eyes. What did Eero see in her?

"So you are a long way from home," she said.

"Yes," I said. "But I was born here."

She responded with a stare. What did she know?

"And you play the piano?" I asked, to be polite.

"Yes," she said. "For many years. I play in the church."

I nodded. This was going to be a long wait. I busied myself sampling the cookies she had put out.

When enough time had passed that I felt she was deliberately trying to make me uncomfortable, I cleared my throat. "What time will my father be home?" I don't know why I said this. I wanted, I suppose, to remind her that I had a right to be there.

"Your father?" she said. She put down her cup on the table as if the weight or the heat of it was suddenly too much.

"Yes," I said. "I know he said he was going to Ivalo today."

"Yes, this is true, but—" She slowed her sentence to a halt. "Excuse me," she said.

She moved into the hallway. Her walk was wide-stanced, but not as absurd as I had imagined. I heard her pick up the phone and say my name. When she hung up, she went to the bathroom and ran the water. I finished my tea and scratched Pia's ears. Could he really not have told her that he and Olivia had had a daughter?

Eero was home in minutes. With two long strides, he was in the living room. He pulled a chair close to me, sat down, and rested his clasped hands on the table. He looked distressed.

"Oh, child," he said. "What does your mother tell you about your father? Who does she say he is?"

I told him that she had told me Richard, her second husband, was my father. But my birth certificate had disclosed the truth: that it was he, Eero.

He said something to himself in his own language. And then he looked at me. "Come with me to the church."

We walked out the door without saying good-bye to Kirsi, who, I gathered, was still in the bathroom. I started to ask Eero a question, but he looked out of sorts, mumbling something. He was, I realized, praying.

9.

We sat in the front pew, and he told me a story, a nasty fairy tale with no moral. In the story, an American woman traveled to Kautokeino, near the town of Masi, to protest the building of a dam that would destroy a Sami village. It was winter and dark, and late one afternoon, while the woman was crossing the frozen Alta River, she was raped.

When she returned home to her husband in Inari, she told him about the rape, and he held her. During the days and the nights, he held her.

The woman didn't want to report the crime, because the man who had raped her was Sami and, at that time in particular, the incident would have been blown out of proportion. The protest was the first thing in her life she had felt connected to.

After seven days, she didn't want to be held anymore. She flinched from her husband, closed doors on him. First, she bathed frequently, and then, after a month, not at all. Her burnished hair turned oily, her slender figure plump.

After three months, the woman told her husband she was with child. They had not been together in the weeks before the trip, nor since her return. She wanted to be rid of the child. She said she felt toxic. That was her word. The husband, who was a religious man and did not believe in abortion, knew that he would die for his wife, if it ever came to that. He said he would raise the child as his own. Together, they would raise the child. No one would know. "Not even God?" the woman said. She practically spit when she said it.

After the child, a daughter, was born, the mother grew belligerent toward her husband. Why had he not gone after the man in Masi? Why had he not been a man? "Because you didn't want me to," he said. But that didn't matter now. "You should have known," the woman screamed, "you shouldn't have let me stop you. I was not in my right mind."

You're not in your right mind now, he wanted to say. But he no longer fought with her.

The priest had been invited to a conference in New Mexico, for indigenous leaders. Eskimo and Native American and Maori priests and politicians and thinkers would be there. He bought a ticket for his wife as well. The child, who was only six months old, would sit on their laps. He believed being in her own country would be good for his wife, that being so far away would be good for them all.

On the third day of the conference, he returned to their room to find the air-conditioning on high and his wife and daughter gone. Their belongings had disappeared with them. The man traveled to his wife's hometown—Davis, California— and rang the doorbells of her sisters' homes. The sisters were stunned by his arrival. The woman, it turned out, had never told her sisters she had married.

10.

I could taste the tears, and I tried to open my mouth, but it was salty and dry, and I had no voice. Eero curved his arm around me, to steady me, as we walked down the aisle of the church, like a couple after a funeral service. "Please, my child, please stay the night."

I thought of his new wife. I couldn't face her; I could barely look at him. I despised him as much as I'd ever despised anyone.

Outside, he turned to lock the door of the church, and I ran in the direction we had come from. I heard him yelling behind me, but I kept running, through town and over the bridge. My backpack thumped against me like a drum.

I was on the other side of the lake when I saw the lights of his car behind me. I ducked into the woods. As I wove between the trees, snow cracked beneath my boots, the sound of light-bulbs burning out. The car slowed and idled, and I stood behind a tree, leaning into it. My eyes had begun to adjust to the darkness, and I saw the small eyes of the trees looking back at me.

"Clarissa," Eero's voice called out. I continued running until I came across a structure. A hut? A teepee? A sign was posted at waist height. TRADITIONAL SAMI LAVU, it read. I looked up and around me, and in the distance saw a large building: the Sami museum. The hut was part of an exhibition.

"Clarissa." Eero's voice echoed. I turned but couldn't see him. Behind me, my footprints appeared as small, dark holes in the snow. I opened the door to the Sami *lavu*, stepped inside, and closed the door.

I inhaled the bosky scent of the bark poles and stood listening for Eero's voice, for the sound of his footsteps. In the distance, a car door slammed. I saw a shadow in the corner of the *lavu*, and took a step back. I pulled the flashlight from my backpack, switched on the beam. It was only another museum sign propped up on a stand. I forced myself to concentrate on reading the words. I needed to anchor my thoughts.

"The Sami *lavu* is the equivalent of the Native American teepee," the sign explained. "The family would sleep in the same *lavu* during reindeer-herding season." A map illustrated who slept where in the *lavu*. The parents slept on one side of the tent, by the kitchen area, and next to them, the smaller children. The hearth was in the center. Past the hearth slept the older children, and beyond them, the servants, who slept by the door.

Now that I was still, I grew cold. Stray strands of hair near my face, wetted by tears, were now frozen. They felt like straw against my cheeks and chin. I crossed my arms and slid my hands under my armpits, the way my mother had taught me. "The warmest part of your body," she'd said.

She had given me so many instructions, instructions that had seemed unprovoked, but now I understood. *If a man tries something on you, force yourself to pee. Use your legs. That's where your weight is. Gouge his eyes with your fingers. Punch his ears with your fists. Ruin his ability to see and hear. And then run.*

Perfume Girl

1.

The summer I was nineteen, I volunteered to work on an archaeological dig in Montana. I read about the project in a paleontology magazine Dad subscribed to. A *T. rex* had been found in the vicinity the year before, and archaeologists were searching for fossils so they could determine when it had lived. I signed up to help, because I liked the photos that accompanied the article. A woman stood in front of a cliff, wielding a pitchfork; a man, arms extended, displayed an unscrolled time line.

The dig had been organized by a paleontologist who had a following among grad students: men with bad posture and delicate fingers, women with pear-shaped bodies and braids. Nonarchaeologists like me included landscapers who wanted to apply their digging skills to science, and middle-aged women who had opted out of their usual Club Med vacations. When I arrived in Montana, I felt adventurous, precocious. I was the youngest volunteer by five or six years.

By that evening, I felt ridiculous, alone. No one had much interest in talking to me. Everyone else teamed up for tents; I was granted my own. It was slick, mildewy, set apart from the others on the side of a dusty hill. At night, I could hear the call of wolves in the distance, and, nearby, the hissing of snakes.

Days at the site were long, the sun high and hot. We spent the first two days chopping down and dragging away the bushes on the site. During the third day, our excavation group scouted out the grounds and superimposed a grid, which we constructed out of six-inch wooden posts and miles of white rope. The rope turned brown after a day.

The seventy volunteers were divided into groups of ten. Matt was my group's supervisor. He was in his late twenties, short but strong, with brown eyes that squinted so you couldn't tell if he was laughing with you or at you. He took off his shirt after ten in the morning and didn't put it back on until night. His spine curved like an *S*.

I was assigned to a plot called G1, four feet by four feet. The real challenge was its depth—I was only allowed to plumb a centimeter at a time. I spent the entirety of one morning sweeping dirt until I found small seashells: Montana used to be underwater.

Matt flirted with the women during lunch at the site, when we relaxed in the shade of a pitched yellow tent. No one bothered to talk to me, except to make sure I was having a good time. A librarian from Idaho checked the inside flap of a book I was reading, to see if I had borrowed it from a library. She had two long hairs hanging from her chin. After I'd finished eating, I would recline on my backpack and pretend to sleep so no one would have to feel bad for me.

Matt would give massages to the women, and, once, to a man. His ex-girlfriend had been a masseuse, he bragged. A masseuse and an archaeologist. I pictured them sitting around giving massages and talking about bones.

On the fourth day of the dig, Matt came by my plot. "How's it going?" he said. I was squatting. He stood above me.

"Okay," I said. I showed him some tiny bones I had come across.

"Fossilized turtle vertebrae," Matt said. "Pretty common."

"Do you think I'll find something big?"

"Sure," he said.

"What's the best thing you've ever found?"

"I was on a dig in New Zealand where we found skeletons." He looked down at his chest and picked something invisible off of it.

"Really?"

"Yeah, I even found the skeleton of a woman and a sheep side by side, like they died fucking."

"Wow," I said and looked at his sandals. He wasn't wearing the snake guards the rest of us wore. His toes were sunburned.

During the second week, Matt told our group that a friend of his who lived in town was having a party. We were all invited. After dinner, our group piled into two cars.

We walked into the kitchen of the house as though best friends, but within a minute, after we'd made ourselves gin and tonics, I found myself alone. The kitchen was crowded with locals, who looked showered. Those of us on the dig bathed in the lake, the dirt trickling down our legs and caking around our ankles.

A hand took my red cup. How could I have already finished my drink? The hand vanished, and a moment later, it re-
appeared.

"The vodka's almost out," said a voice. Matt. "Getting you a
refill while there's still some left."

"It was gin," I said, taking a sip of the new, stronger drink.

He shrugged. He was wearing a sweatshirt that said COLLEGE.

"So what's your number?" he said.

"My number?"

"Yeah, how many countries have you been to?"

I tried to suppress a laugh. "Counting America, one."

He had asked me the question so I would ask him. He
was waiting. "And you?" I said. "What's your—" I paused—
"number?"

"Sixteen," he said. "But I've only been to four continents.
So far."

He told me a story about a Turkish bath in Istanbul, where
he'd gone with his ex-girlfriend. She got felt up. "Not by me,"
he added. He looked like he needed to spit.

We had somehow moved into a corner of the kitchen. I
spotted a mousetrap on the floor by the stove, near his feet.

"Watch out," I said, and pointed.

He took a step away from the mousetrap, closer to me.

"I like the little gap between your teeth," he said.

"They've been trying to put me in braces my whole life," I
said, liking that he had noticed.

I felt emboldened by the gin. "I like your muscles," I said.

"Yeah?" he said. "All the better to hold you with."

"Who *are* you? The wolf in *Red Riding Hood*?"

"Whoever you want me to be. What else do you like?"

"I like your voice." I wanted to feel the strength that came with giving compliments.

"What do you like about it?"

"It's very commanding," I said. But I wasn't sure this was what I liked, or that I liked it at all.

"Kiss me," he said, a bit too forcefully.

"I don't know," I said.

"Oh, come on," he said. "As the man says, I don't want to wait in vain for your love."

"The man?"

"Bob Marley."

I laughed. "I didn't realize you were waiting in vain. I thought we were having a conversation."

"Do you have a boyfriend?" he said angrily. "Is that it?" Suddenly his mouth was inches from my face, his breath reeking of scotch.

"Yes," I lied, and took another sip of my drink. I was holding it between us like a shield.

"That's unfortunate."

"Unfortunate?" I asked. I wasn't feeling well. The lights in the kitchen were too bright.

"What's his name?"

"Whose?"

"Your boyfriend."

"James," I said. Did I know anyone named James? I couldn't remember.

"That's my real name," he said. His mouth was open, mocking.

"What?"

"It's James Matthew," he said.

He signaled to his friend across the room. I didn't recognize him from the dig, and figured he lived in town. He was tall, with a straight nose and wide sideburns that didn't match his hair.

"Listen to this, Kurt," Matt said. "Clarissa here says I'm her boyfriend."

"That was fast," Kurt said. "How quickly you two have become acquainted."

Who talked like that? I tried to think of what to say to make things normal again, but my mind was a parachute that had failed to open.

"Something's not right," I said.

"Maybe it's your perfume," Kurt said. "It's too strong. What's a nice girl like you doing wearing perfume like that?"

"I don't wear perfume," I said.

I parted them with my hands, like a swimmer, and went outside. I left the house, the screen door slapping behind me. I felt warm in the cold that hit Montana at night. I hitched a ride back to where I was staying. It wasn't far—five, ten minutes. The driver turned on the windshield wipers to clear the dust and dropped me off at the base of the campground. I hopped through the tall grass; I wasn't wearing my snake guards.

None of the tents around mine seemed occupied. I lay down in my sleeping bag and held my head in my hands to keep it steady. It was either ten minutes or an hour later that I heard my tent being unzipped.

"Wrong tent," I called out.

"Hello perfume," they said.

2.

There had been a joke about the hair on my spine. Something about an armadillo—who was talking to whom? Was he talking to me? Were there two of them? It hurt to open my eyes, it hurt to close them.

I remember him rolling on me, into me, my wrists stiff above my head—were they tied? *I'm being punished*, I thought. I had said daring things, gone too far with my flattery. Up until tonight, I had rarely given compliments. And now I had over-compensated.

3.

I woke the next morning and stared at the zipper to the tent. It was open an inch at its base.

Until that night, I had been a virgin. *I'm involved with some-one; he lives in Texas.*

4.

It hurt too much to use a tampon. I put on all my pairs of underwear to stop the bleeding.

5.

I stuck my head outside. The tent had slipped ten feet down the hill.

I pulled myself back inside and zipped the tent shut.

For the first time in years, I related to Jeremy's quiet. It was too difficult, too much to speak.

I didn't want to press charges. I didn't want to be the girl who had been raped. I didn't want to leave the dig. I didn't want Dad to think I couldn't be on my own. I didn't want other people to think I had been too young, after all. I didn't want to do anything.

6.

I stood in the *lavu*, hands curled into my armpits, unsure of when it was safe to leave.

How rarely I thought of that night now. The thumbprint bruises faded in nine days. As I bathed in the lake, I'd watched them change from purple to green to brown. *Why are you fighting? Be a lover, not a fighter.*

After a decade, strong scents still made a fist of my stomach. It didn't matter what the source was: Casablanca lilies, potpourri, eucalyptus in a steam room. Magazines arrived in the mail, and I ripped out the fragranced pages, discarded them in the building's foyer. Pankaj bought me a perfume he liked. I sniffed it to be polite but never wore it. The one time I met his ex-girlfriend, she was wearing the same scent.

Now, as I stood in the *lavu*, I began picturing that night, the red cup, the mousetrap, the sideburns. I saw the arm pinned to the floor of the tent, but it wasn't mine. It was my mother's. When I pictured a leg, a thumb pressing into the thigh, it was her leg, her kneecap with its sharp blond hairs. It was her I heard softly protest as the man placed her hands above her head, locking her down, thrusting.

I fell to my knees. I rested my forehead on the *lavu* floor, covered with reindeer skin, and wept. I tried to pray. *Forgive me*, I said. *Forgive me.*

Northern Lights

1.

I left the *lavu*, closing the door behind me, and followed my footsteps back to the road. There was no sign of Eero Valkeapää or his Volvo, no sign that anyone was awake. Inari was still, like a city the night after a bombing. I tightened the straps of my backpack and ran again.

From a drawer beneath the cabin's kitchen sink I took out a knife, still with butter on its teeth. I sat at the kitchen table, the knife to my right. I turned the blade so it was facing me, as though I was setting a table for company. Then I turned the blade outward. Inward, outward, inward, outward.

2.

I sat upright in the wooden chair for hours, waiting for the night to pass. I took out the five photos of my mother and spread them around the table. Moving from chair to chair, I examined each one.

I would go to Kautokeino, where my mother had stayed, and then to Masi, where the act had taken place. I never wanted to see Inari again.

What would Eero and Kirsi say about me to each other? To them, I would be the girl who wanted so badly to believe.

3.

I woke with my face on one of my mother's portraits. I had slept forehead-to-forehead with her.

It was eight a.m. when I left the cabin for the bus station, my suitcase dragging behind me like a child's sled. When I arrived at the station, Eero was there, standing in front of his car.

"I want to say good-bye," he said.

"How did you know what time I was leaving?"

"I wait since morning."

"But how did you know I was leaving today?" I said.

"You are your mother's daughter." A cruel thing to say.

"Did you know the man's name, the man in Masi?"

Eero shook his head, and averted his eyes, looking at the ground. "No."

I wasn't sure I believed him.

He stepped forward to hug me good-bye, and I grew tense, feverish. I was sweating in the cold. I unfolded myself from his embrace. *Two. I have now mistakenly believed two men to be my father. Never again.*

I lifted my suitcase into the luggage mouth of the bus to Helsinki. I had packed the knife in the bag, thinking I might have to use it should I find the man who had raped my mother. It was best if Eero didn't know where I was going.

Eero turned and walked back to his Volvo. As he started the car, I could hear the radio, the volume turned high, playing the same song I'd heard on the bus with Kari, the song about driving home for Christmas. When Eero and the Volvo were down the road, I pulled my suitcase off the Helsinki-bound bus and loaded it onto the one going north.

4.

On the way out of town, the bus passed a sign. A rendering of a city—church steeple, high-rise buildings—with a red slash through it. We had left Inari. It looked nothing like the sign.

In the distance, a white circle hung in the sky, like a halo. The sun? It was so low down on the horizon, it was hard to tell. It could easily be the light of a distant lamppost.

Snow dropped, first thick, then wet. The bus driver turned on the large windshield wipers. A soothing, metronome sound. My heartbeat slowed to match the rhythm, and soon I felt myself on the cliff of sleep.

How obvious: I dreamed of my mother. In the dream, she was the age I was now, wearing the clothes I last saw her in. The suede pants faded at the lap creases. The black sweater that made her chest look like a shelf. She was sitting on the frozen Alta River, salt and pepper poured onto it like sand. She'd written something in the seasoning, and I leaned over her shoulder to see: TOXIC.

5.

Karasjok, Norway. The hum of the bus came to a groan. I checked with the woman at the ticket counter. I had missed the bus to Kautokeino. "Ten minutes ago," she said. With her hand, she simulated an airplane taking off.

The next bus wasn't for two hours. I felt like a shattered window—at any moment, at the slightest provocation, the pieces would fall to the ground, hard as hail.

At the bus station newsstand, I bought a bag of licorice and a phone card. I paid with euros, and got kroner in change. I had crossed the Norwegian border.

The next bus came, and as I boarded, I felt faint. Sugar, I needed sugar. The licorice I had bought was frozen, unchewable

The bus slowed and stopped; three animals were blocking the road. Reindeer. They were smaller than horses, their antlers delicate. Mythical-looking creatures, wearing white ankle socks. The bus driver honked until the reindeer sprinted out of the way. To steady my head and my stomach, I clutched the back of the seat in front of me, its upholstery tacky, bright. Animals in the road reminded me of Taft, the cat my mother had adopted as her own. The cat that, three years after my mother vanished, I killed with my car. An accident, I said.

6.

The woman sitting in the seat across the bus's aisle was scratching her lottery ticket with the tips of a bobby pin. Could she—could everyone—tell there was something wrong with me? Was I convulsing or talking out loud? I feared that I had crossed to the other side without realizing it. I stared down at my hands to see if they were quivering. They were steady, but something was different, my fingers more bare. My engagement ring—where was it? For almost a year I had worn it, and now it was gone.

I searched my pants pockets, my coat. I dug through the compartments of my backpack. I turned my left glove inside out and pulled at the fingers one by one, as though counting mistakes. "Stupid, stupid, stupid, stupid," I said.

The woman with the lottery ticket looked over at me and quickly turned away.

7.

The bus driver told me there weren't any hotels in Masi, only something called a "field house" in Kautokeino, the closest town. It was where Eero said my mother had stayed. I got off in Kautokeino and walked down the side of the main road. There was still light, and in the distance, I could see a church with a cross. The town looked like Bethlehem on Christmas.

I followed signs up a hill to the field house. Once inside the heavy doors, I called out. I was out of breath from the climb, from the cold. A thin man in his forties came to meet me. His name was Nils, and he seemed surprised I was alone, and more surprised that I was American. "You look Sami," he said.

"Thank you," I said. "You have a room?"

8.

It had been decorated for summer. The comforter, patterned with orange poppies, was the texture of paper towels. I placed my head on the pillow, and only when lying down did I acknowledge that I was dizzy, my nose moist. I sat up. I had no time to be sick.

It was a little after one p.m., which meant it was morning in New York. I dialed Jeremy and felt a pang of homesickness for the way the phone rang. I got Dede, the nurse on duty—one whose face I couldn't place among the Greek chorus of nurses.

"He's fine," Dede said. No accent, a source of irrational relief. "Just fine." She said Jeremy hadn't had an episode since the night of the funeral. I asked to be put on the phone with him, but Dede said he was sleeping. "Can you call back in half an hour or so?"

I stared at the phone. I wanted someone to call. I had to remind myself Dad was not an option.

I chewed on my thawed licorice. When the bag was finished, I tried calling Jeremy again. A nurse named Laura answered. I knew her! She had piercings all the way up both ears, but wore no jewelry on her wrists or hands. She gave me an update and put Jeremy on. I heard his loud breathing. "Hi honey," I said. "I'm in Lapland." I made it sound like it was a vacation destination, some place I'd long dreamed of traveling to. I was careful whenever speaking with Jeremy, fearful that one day he would start talking and he would laugh and make it clear that he had understood everything I had ever said, everything anyone had ever said. "I've been quiet my whole life," he would explain, "because talking seemed like it would complicate things."

We were on the phone for ten minutes. I wrapped up my monologue. "I love you, Jeremy," I said. Never so much as a grunt of acknowledgment. Not before, and not today. "Did you hear me?" I said. "Did you *fucking* hear me?"

Laura was back on the phone. "Are you talking to me?" she asked.

I hung up.

9.

I brushed my teeth, emptied my backpack, and repacked it with my wallet, the photos of my mother, and the knife. In the reception area, I looked for Nils. I wanted to show him the photos, to ask him questions. But he was nowhere, and I didn't want to ring the doorbell to what I saw must be his living quarters. No other room had a doorbell.

I zipped up my coat and set out with no plan in mind. Once outside, I unzipped my coat, removed my hat—was it warm out? I half-walked, half-slid down the hill to the main road. Teenage boys on snowmobiles sped past like bees. Older women in local Sami outfits, all wearing red hats, were gathered outside a grocery store.

"Excuse me," I said. I removed a photo of my mother from the envelope. "Did you happen to know this woman?" The photo was passed from small hand to small hand. I took out all the photos so each of the five women had her own.

One woman, the shortest of the short group, said something to the others. Then she spoke to me in Sami. It was clear the women didn't speak any English, or understand a word I was saying. And yet, the more confused they looked, the more I talked. "She was living here while taking part in the early Alta Dam protests," I said. "She was American, one of the only ones involved. Did you know her?"

The shortest woman pointed down the road. "Alta," she said. The others joined in. "Alta Dam," they said, nodding. One of them pointed to the bus stop.

"Thank you," I said.

For a moment, I felt we were all related, the five Sami women and I. None of us understood anything.

10.

The sky was now muted, the town cast in a flesh tone. I wasn't feeling well—my legs pulsed with fatigue, black spots floated in front of my eyes. *I can sleep tonight*, I told myself. I continued walking up the road until I got to a gas station with a small market. Suddenly hungry, I scoured the store for snacks. It was stocked with shelves of flashlights and stuffed animals, most of them tigers. Next to the tigers, a bin of Sami hats—red, bulbous like pincushions.

The cashier was an older man in a Sami tunic that fit him

like a dress. Beneath the tunic he wore motorcycle pants. I took out the photos.

"I was curious if you ever knew this woman? She was here during the Alta Dam protests, staying in this town."

The man took the photos in his hand and leafed through them slowly. I appreciated how delicately he handled them.

"I don't think I remember," he said. Two men walked into the store, and he greeted them by name—Henrik and something else. Everyone in the town knew each other.

"She was American, maybe that helps," I said.

"It was a very long time ago," he said, and he handed the photos back to me. He looked at me with concern. "You are okay?" he asked.

"Yes," I said. I wondered what he was seeing.

The men he had addressed approached the counter. They were young, in their early twenties.

"What are the pictures of?" one of them said to me. His English was good.

"Oh," I said, looking at the photo on top of the stack. My mother had a mole on her collarbone, something I hadn't noticed before, or had forgotten. "I was curious if anyone knew anything about this woman. She was here a long time ago. You're too young to have known her."

The man had blondish hair and smelled like cold. He stood next to me, shoulder-to-shoulder, and examined the photos, as though we were friends sharing pictures after a trip.

"She looks like you," he said.

"Really?" No one had ever told me that before.

"Yeah, the shape of her eyes. I'm Henrik," he said. He had a smile that started slowly and spread from the right side of his face to the left.

"Clarissa." I didn't want the conversation to end. "How did you learn English?"

"I've spent a lot of time in Barcelona," he said.

Henrik's friend was buying tobacco and rolling paper. Henrik called out to him, and the friend picked up another package of tobacco.

"Nice to meet you," Henrik said.

"Likewise," I said.

"Like what?"

"Nothing. Nice meeting you," I said. I blushed and turned toward the door. I had been dismissed, but I didn't want to leave. I didn't want to be alone again.

"Welcome to beautiful Kautokeino," Henrik called after me. "Kautokeino welcomes you."

I waved.

Outside, at the gas station pumps, I saw the men's snow-mobiles. Whom did Henrik remind me of? No one. He seemed familiar because I wanted to know him.

11.

I walked to the bus stop, waited, and boarded a bus going to Masi. Outside, the sky turned the sherbet colors of Hawaiian hotels. My mind was deceiving me: if I squinted, a snow field became a beach.

I held my mother's photos between my hands the way I would a map. "When I gave birth to you," my mother once said to me, "it felt like someone was stabbing me with a knife."

The bus let me out at the turnoff to Masi. The town, from what I could see, was to the north of the bus stop, on a sloping hill. I started down the road, past the modest one-story houses. Most homes had a car in the driveway, a simple strand of Christmas lights outlining a door. Through one lit window, I saw twin girls practicing cartwheels.

I had thought that I'd be looking for a person, not a place, but now that I was here, I found myself walking slightly faster downhill, toward the clearing. I assumed it was the Alta River, though now it was covered with snow. I approached the river, and the road took a turn. I followed it, passing larger two-story houses, and, on my left, a white wooden church. It was the first building I'd seen in this town that wasn't a home—there appeared to be no restaurants, stores, bars.

Turning off the road, I followed a set of snowmobile tracks that cut through the riverbank. I was cautious of slipping—the grooves had turned icy, but the only alternative was to walk in the snow, which was too deep. It had been a mistake to wear such tractionless boots.

A brown car was parked on the side of the river. Empty. I tightened the forgotten scarf around my neck and tucked the ends into the top of my coat. I had been lucky to find the scarf. "Lucky," I said to myself, and laughed.

I took a tentative step onto the ice. It was covered in a foot of snow. If the ice could support so much snow, I thought, it could support me. In my scarf, in my jacket, I was invincible.

I walked farther out onto the river. *It happened there*, I thought, looking in one direction. I turned. *Or there.* I turned again and again and again. I faced the darkness of the trees on the other side of the river. *Or there.*

As I turned, still looking for the site of the act, the site of my conception, I grew dizzy. I heard wobbling sounds above me, around me, in my head. My ears were so alert I could hear sound waves. Bolts of light shot across the night. I collapsed onto the frozen river, my eyes staring up at the crackling sky. It was lit like an aquarium.

I tried to use my hands to push myself up to a sitting position. They slipped on the ice. Something was wrong with me. I felt weak and energetic at the same time. I could knock down a house with my bare hands if I wanted to. I could scream and crack open the sky. I laughed at the thought. Beneath my head, the ice felt as hot as lava.

This Is How to Prove a Reindeer Belongs to You

1.

A man in a red jacket was squatting down beside me. He took off a glove and reached for my face. I blocked his hand with my arm.

"*Nej,*" he said. "*Nej, nej.*" He put his fingers to his forehead. He'd been trying to feel my temperature.

He turned his head toward a shape, another figure. My legs tensed, and I took in a quick breath. Then I heard a woman's voice. She knelt and looked into me, a befuddled expression on her face. They took turns talking to me, one sentence at a time.

"I don't know," I said. "I don't understand." It was only then that I knew where I was.

"English?" the woman said to me.

"American," I said.

"Yes, but you speak English?"

"English, yes," I said.

I felt hands behind my back, propping me up. "Water," the woman said, and a moment later, cold liquid filled my mouth. I choked before asking for more.

They spoke quickly to each other. Sami. Lifting me to my feet, they placed their arms around my shoulders, palms on my elbows, and walked me in the direction of a car. The brown one I'd seen parked by the river earlier.

"What time?" I said.

"Five in the morning," said the woman.

They put me in the front seat and turned on the heater. My hands and nose itched from the hot air. "Enough," I said. "No."

"Where are you staying?" the woman asked.

"The field house," I said, proud that I remembered. Relieved that they seemed to understand. I gathered that the man was Ailo, and that he wasn't as confident of his English as the woman. Janne.

Janne drove, and Ailo sat in the backseat. I tried to stay awake, but my head was dense. I looked out the window. I thought we'd been driving for an hour, but we weren't yet up the hill. The tires of the car seemed airless. We were too low to the ground.

I unbuckled my belt. My head pulsed. I reached up to remove the rubber band that I was sure I had fastened too tight, but there wasn't one—my hair was loose. My head pulsed harder. I had the terrifying sensation that everything coming back to me now—*Eero wasn't my father; my mother had been raped*—might be true.

We parked outside the field house, and Ailo ventured out to open the front door. It was locked. He returned to the car and discussed the situation with Janne. I interpreted *coffee*, I interpreted *hospital*. I understood that Ailo was more concerned about me than Janne was. He was for the hospital, while she was advocating food.

"Are you hungry?" Janne asked.

"Yes," I said. I wasn't sure if I was hungry, but I didn't want them to leave me. He was gentle; I liked the way he unscrewed the water bottle each time I wanted to take a sip. She was determined—you could see her strength in her angular features, you could hear it in her voice. Together they could raise me. This idea was pleasing, soothing, until it occurred to me that I was older than they were. For a moment, I'd believed I was a teenager. That I was fourteen, eighteen.

Janne got out of the car—a gust of cold—and walked around the field house. She stopped at a door on the side. The owner, Nils, emerged in his pajamas. He disappeared and, a moment later, opened the front door.

Janne and Ailo ushered me inside. Nils apologized for locking me out. "I thought you were in bed," he said. I, too, thought it was his fault that I had been in the cold all night, before I remembered. And then I willed myself to forget. The man seemed to know Ailo and Janne; together they discussed what to do with me. Janne removed her glove and felt my forehead with the back of her hand. She said something to the others, and turned to me. "High fever," she pronounced.

Nils and Ailo searched for food, and Janne led me to my room. "Nils says a phone call came for you last night," Janne said. "Apparently you were showing pictures?"

I nodded. I was sitting on the bed, on the summer comforter. Janne sat in a chair, with her thin legs crossed, a formal position for so early in the morning. She took off her hat. She wore her brown hair in three short braids.

"The man who called said he met you. Henrik?"

I remembered and nodded. Words were difficult. My tongue lay thick and too far back in my mouth.

"Yes, he is a friend of mine, too," she said. "His aunt is very well known here. She is a healer. She heard you were showing pictures. She believes she can help."

"A healer?"

"Yes, but not a witch doctor. We were talking now, Nils and Ailo and me, how maybe you should go to her. Since she already offered."

"I'd like to stay here and sleep," I said.

"That's the other thing," Janne said. "Nils says he's booked tonight. You have to move out."

Nils was lying.

"Okay," I said. "I'll go to the healer." Strange words to say.

"Good," she said and looked at her watch. "I'll call Henrik in an hour, when it's not so early, and tell him. Why don't you rest until he gets here?"

2.

I awoke to a knock at the door: Henrik.

"So we meet again," he said. Around his neck, he wore a black rope necklace with a silver pendant the shape of an animal tooth.

I tried to speak but grunted instead.

"I'm going to take you to my aunt," he said. "Her name

is Anna Kristine. She wanted to help you yesterday, when she heard you had lost someone."

I nodded. I had lost someone.

"I brought my scooter," Henrik said. "I don't have a car. Do you think you're strong enough to hold on?"

"Yes," I lied.

Henrik carried my suitcase outside and placed it in the storage compartment of a snowmobile. Nils wished me well; he looked relieved.

"It's not far," Henrik said. He sat down in front of me on the snowmobile, and I wrapped my arms around his puffy jacket. As we drove through the wind, my eyes bled water. Within minutes, we approached a small red house. It was surrounded by other houses, also red. Henrik helped me off the snowmobile.

I followed him up three stairs. Inside—a rush of heat and an old woman sitting on a couch, knitting. "This is Anna Kristine," Henrik said.

She stood and moved toward me. If I hadn't seen her face, etched by age and cold, I would have thought she was a child. She was four and a half feet tall.

I lost my legs. I fell against Henrik, spiraled to the floor. There were palms upon me, so many fingers.

They led me into a small, dark bedroom, and I toppled on a mattress. Anna Kristine said something to Henrik, and he left the room. She peeled off my pants, long underwear, and socks, and dressed me in a flannel nightgown and knitted slippers.

After ten minutes, or twenty, Henrik returned to the room

with a coffee cup. He propped me up and held the cup to my lips. I took a big sip and nearly choked.

The liquid was viscous, salty, neither cold nor hot. "What is it?"

"Reindeer blood," Henrik said. "My aunt asked me to bring some to you."

"No," I said, pushing away the cup.

"You're sick," he said, "and she's trying to make you good. The blood is good for chills."

He held the cup up to my mouth again, and I made myself swallow. "It tastes like electricity," I whispered to no one in particular.

Strands of hair stuck to my forehead. I was sweating. Anna Kristine's weathered fingers smoothed the strands from my face and tucked them behind my ears. I grasped her hand and held it tightly.

"Don't leave," I said.

3.

I woke alone. The room was small, with a single bed and a dresser. Anna Kristine's daughter's room. Old dolls sat bowed and tilted in the corner, like paralyzed children robbed of their wheelchairs. A silver thimble and a brooch lay on the bedside table, next to a clock that had stopped. It was the kind of room from which everything important has been packed up, shipped off.

I called out and was surprised by the sound of my own voice. It was soft and desperate. Anna Kristine came to my side. She rotated my ankles. She pressed lightly on all sides of my stomach, and examined my tongue. On my forehead, she placed a washcloth, and on my calf and against the back of my head, she pressed strips of what looked like bark.

Henrik brought me toast, and I ate four bites hungrily. "What's the bark for?" I asked.

"To stop the bleeding," he said, without consulting Anna Kristine. "She did the same thing to me when I was young." He pushed up the sleeve of his heavy gray sweater and showed me a small scar.

"My head is bleeding?" I said.

"Just a little. You bumped it, yes?"

I nodded, and raised my hand to touch my head. Anna Kristine caught my wrist and guided my arm back down to my side. She said something to Henrik.

"She says you are suffering from shock, from exhaustion, from chills. She'd like you to stay here for a few days until you get better, you see," he said. "I live next door if you need a translator. This is okay?"

"I'm sorry," I said.

He smiled weakly.

Neither of them had asked me what I was doing on the frozen Alta River. For this, I loved them more. I felt something on my lips and saw that Anna Kristine was applying Vaseline.

"You're too kind," I said. I meant it.

4.

I fell asleep at 12:00 and I awoke when my watch read 4:10. I woke again at 5:20 and 6:05, but whether it was day or night I did not know—the curtains were heavy, the sky the colors of an ocean floor.

5.

I woke up sweating between my breasts. I blotted myself dry with a sock.

Nightmares suffused my sleep. In one, there were too many people in the bed: my mother, Pankaj, Virginia—and the man who raped my mother. I crawled to the corner of the mattress, careful not to touch any of them.

My mind traveled to the narrow bed of my childhood room, where there was only room for me. I watched everyone else tumble off the side and roll behind the ruffled bed skirt. They remained there along with old files, torn ski pants, a crushed game of Risk.

6.

Anna Kristine's legs were short beneath her dress. She floated into my room occasionally with water, and tea, and two types of bread: crisp and soft.

"I'm so sorry," I told her. "I'll be out of here by tomorrow."

I was reminded of Kari, of having to watch over him, the nuisance of it all.

"Shhh," she said. She couldn't understand what I was saying. I didn't think I'd ever been so close to someone so old. Her eyes were the soft brown of suede, and her breath was sweet, as if exhaling air from a happier time.

7.

A man stood in the doorway of the room, watching me. Henrik.

"How long has it been?" I asked.

"Two days," he said.

"I'm sorry to be so much trouble."

"No trouble," he said. "My aunt likes you."

"Thank you for bringing me here." I couldn't look at him when I said this. There were many things I wanted to ask him, but I said nothing.

Henrik sat down in the chair next to the bed. His skin was wind-chafed, his lips full. He began to talk about reindeer.

"For the past two days I've been out with my reindeer," he said. "But I'll be around more in the coming days. If you need anything."

"Reindeer?" I said. My voice was sore, deep.

He closed his eyes to say yes.

"How many do you have?" I didn't know why I cared.

"Between two thousand and twelve thousand," he said.

I mumbled something about being impressed.

"Can I tell you a secret?" he said. I nodded gravely, wanting his secret. "You don't ask a Sami how many reindeer he owns. It's like me asking you how much money is in your bank account."

"I'm sorry," I said. A second later, I understood what he meant. "Do you use a snowmobile to herd them?"

"Yes, that's how I move them down from the mountains. I use a scooter—that's what we call snowmobile."

"What did herders do before snowmobiles? Skis?" I wanted to force my thoughts onto something other than Richard, Pankaj, my mother, the man.

"Yes, skis," Henrik said.

I stared at the knife hanging from his waist in what looked like a holster. "Do you kill them with that?"

"This is for grouse, this knife. And for marking the reindeer. Everyone marks the ears of their reindeer," he said. He searched his pocket for a pen, and then looked around the room for paper. On the back of an unused envelope, he drew two ears. "This is the left," he said as he made two triangle-shaped slits. "And here, in the right, are three cuts, but higher." He made the slashes quickly and without hesitation, the way some people write their signature. It was his mark.

Only people whose grandparents had herded reindeer were allowed to own them, he told me. In Norway, there were only five hundred permits given out, one permit per family. "I come from a big family of reindeer herders, you see," he said. "Wait here, I'll show you."

8.

I smoothed down my hair and rose higher up on the bed, my pillow propped behind me.

Henrik returned to the room and sat down in the chair, a photo album in his lap. He handed me a small paperback book.

"It's the directory of all the reindeer herders' markings," he said. The book was arranged alphabetically by family name. He took the book, flipped to *Nilssen*, and handed it back to me. There were nine entries.

"That's your last name?" I said.

He nodded.

The directory listed each person's name within the family, what town they lived in, what markings were on the reindeers' left and right ears.

He pointed to his sister's mark, his mother's, his aunt's, his brother's. His sister lived in Oslo now, and didn't herd anymore; she had sold her reindeer to Henrik.

"So your family has always lived in Kautokeino?" I asked.

"Yes," he said. "I also brought some pictures of the trip to our island, you see."

"No, I don't see," I said.

He looked at me.

"I'm teasing you. Your English is very good. But you don't have to say *you see* all the time. People don't do that."

"I see," he said and smiled. "Thank you." Then he told me about his family's island.

9.

The island was off the west coast of Norway. Many herders preferred to keep their animals on an island; it was easier to contain them. The reindeer migrated toward the coast in the spring anyway, driven by mosquitoes and attracted by the coast's cooler climate. The reindeer lived on the island until fall, when they were led back to Kautokeino.

Henrik was sitting close to me, as though he was telling me a bedtime story. He smelled like a hamster I used to own.

The album was decorated with beach balls. Each ball was a different color—pink, blue, yellow. The first photo was of his family packing the sleighs, preparing to lead the reindeer from Kautokeino to the water. "That's me," he said, pointing to a boy of about nine.

I looked at him, and then at the photo. He had the same wide, crooked smile.

"And there's Anna Kristine," he said, pointing to another picture. The photo was taken inside a *lavu*. She looked like she was waking up, with blankets still covering her legs. I stared at the picture, did my math. Even when she was younger, she looked old.

"Anna Kristine was with you? Did your whole family go?" I had spent a total of four afternoons with my aunts in California. Women who drank copious amounts of tea and wore large, dangling pendants. I couldn't fathom going on a trip with them.

"Yes, everyone, every year. It takes six weeks to get out to the coast, sometimes more, in the spring. Then six weeks to get back to Kautokeino in the fall."

I returned my eyes to the photo album.

"And here's a photo," he said excitedly, "of a reindeer giving birth. Usually they give birth on the island and then the babies have all summer to grow strong and fat before we lead them to Kautokeino. But this one gave birth early, while we were still on the journey out to the coast."

"So you put the baby on the sleigh for the rest of the trip?"

"No, we leave them behind."

"Alone?"

"Yes, but they catch up eventually. The mother waits for the calf to get stronger, you see. And then she leads it to the island. They know how to get there even when we're out of sight."

"But how do they know how to get across the water?" I asked. I was looking at another picture, this one of hundreds of reindeer boarding a large boat that would take them to the island. It was the kind of boat I'd seen take cars across water, but never animals. We both stared at the picture. "How do the mother and child get across without the boat? Does it come back for them?"

Henrik shook his head. "They swim to the island," he said. "They know."

Since I was young, I'd been interested in stories of mothers and children. After hearing them, I'd determine whether or not they applied to my mother and me.

Henrik's reindeer story didn't help me at all.

10.

A number of pictures had been removed from the album. Hardened glue that once ran the periphery of the photos, holding them in place, now outlined their absence.

Henrik skipped ahead to pictures of the family leading the reindeer back in the fall. The reindeer were bigger, stronger, and the herders wore lighter clothing—floral dresses, shorts. Everyone was smiling, laughing. A thousand wrinkles in the sun.

"Do you dye your hair blond?" I asked. In his childhood photos, his hair was brown.

"No," Henrik said.

"Oh," I said. "I thought maybe you did. Everyone else in your family has dark hair."

"My mother dyes it," Henrik said.

"Your mother dyes her hair?"

"No," he said. "My mother dyes my hair."

Henrik continued talking, pointing, but now I was weak again. My eyelids were heavy and stayed closed for a moment too long. Henrik must have noticed—he took the glass of water from my hand before I spilled.

"Sweet dreams," he said.

For all I knew, it was morning.

11.

Anna Kristine woke me up and led me down the hall to another bathroom, this one with a tub. She helped me undress. I slid into the porcelain tub, and she left me alone. Sinking lower, I studied my legs under the surface. Bruises on the thigh and calf. I couldn't remember how or why. Black hairs in every direction. It had been so long since I'd had leg hair I didn't know what it would look like. I traced a hand over my leg, upwards. It was sharp, somehow pleasurable.

Pankaj liked to shave my legs. The first time he shaved them, he had come into the bathroom to talk. While sitting on the side of the tub, without a word, he lifted my right foot to the edge and lathered my leg. He shaved it well, quiet and methodical. When he was done, he put his hand on my heel and lowered my leg into the bath. Then he lifted the other one.

I sank into Anna Kristine's bathtub until the water came to my ears. Under the surface, the sounds of tunnels.

Anna Kristine returned to the bathroom and frowned when she saw me. I had gotten my hair wet. She wrapped it in a towel and sighed. With rough strokes, she ran a comb with small teeth through my thick hair. I had underestimated her strength.

12.

I felt well enough to dress and walk back to my room. Anna Kristine had remade the bed with fresh, crisp sheets. I slipped into them and closed my eyes.

Between naps, a small girl stared at me from the chair. She was maybe five years old, with wide eyes and a plump upper lip. She was not real. I was prone to hallucinations while sick; I turned over and went back to sleep.

I woke up again, and still she was there, on the chair, removing a Band-Aid from her elbow. I didn't know how she'd gotten into the room, or how long she'd been watching me.

I waved to her, and she waved back. In my sleep, I'd twisted and kicked my new bedding down to my feet. The girl slipped off the chair and pulled up the sheet, then the blanket, and then the bedspread, and tucked me in.

"Thank you," I said, and coughed. From the bedside table, she handed me the glass of water, now full again, and I took a sip. When I handed it back to her, she tried to match her own fingerprints to the ones I had left on the glass.

"What's your name?" I said.

The girl giggled. From her shoulder hung a purse shaped like a clock. The time on the clock was ten after ten. From inside the purse, she pulled a book and began to sing a lullaby. I didn't understand a word, but I nearly cried. I looked at the cover; the book was turned upside down.

13.

Later, I was awake, and the girl was gone.

I put my hands between my legs and then on my stomach. A calendar hung from a wall. As I pulled it down, a thumbtack fell to the floor.

I turned the calendar pages backwards from December. I

counted and counted again. Seven weeks had passed since my last period.

It had been the night Pankaj and I went to see *The Ice Man Cometh* at a theater downtown. The play was long, three hours, and awful, and he convinced me to walk out before intermission.

"Your job," he said, "has made you immune to bad art."

We stopped at a used bookstore on the way home, and Pankaj bought a paperback of the play. On the subway, he skimmed through it and dog-eared the scene where we'd walked out.

At home, we climbed to the roof and sat on a slowly deflating air mattress. We'd left it there in August, during the heat wave, and now it was fall. We kept our coats on. "Do you want to sit on my lap and talk about the first thing that comes up?"

It was a dumb joke. He had said it several times to me, and, I was sure, to other women before.

"Shut up," I said, and pulled up my skirt. I wrapped my legs around him, crossing my ankles at the base of his spine.

14.

Anna Kristine set the dinner table for the two of us. My first meal out of bed. She handed me matches to light the candles, and served us each a bowl of stew. I looked away as she hoisted herself up onto her seat. The chairs were of average height.

I took a spoonful of the stew. The taste of reindeer.

"It's good," I said, and smiled.

She smiled back.

"Anna Kristine," I said. "I'm pregnant." I gestured with my hands to indicate a protruding belly.

It took her a moment to understand what I was saying, that I wasn't full. "Yes," she said, and nodded. She pointed to her temple and then to her eye, and then to her temple. She'd known that first night.

She rose from the table and returned with a picture of herself, taken maybe fifty years earlier. In the photo, she was reclining on one of the sleighs the family used when leading the reindeer to the island. The sleigh was the shape of a small boat. She was wearing a bright, floral-patterned housedress that stretched across a pregnant stomach. Her hands rested on top of the mound, clasped and proud.

"Daughter?" I said.

She stared at me. I pointed at the picture again, at her stomach. "Your daughter?" I said.

She shook her head no.

I motioned to Anna Kristine to excuse me for a moment. I retrieved the photos of my mother from my backpack. I had never shown them to Anna Kristine, only to Henrik. I selected my favorite one and held it out to her.

"My mother," I said.

Anna Kristine nodded as I handed it to her.

"Do you recognize her?" I said.

Anna Kristine didn't answer. She seemed to see something in the picture.

"Did you know her?" I said. I gestured toward her and then to the photo. I held my breath.

Anna Kristine shook her head no.

15.

After dinner, sadness surrounded Anna Kristine. We sat in front of the TV, watching *Fanny and Alexander*. I tried to follow the plot, while Anna Kristine repaired her shoes. They were pointed at the tips, like elf slippers. She was sitting still, a vague look in her eye. To the right of her head, a doorknob jutted out from the wall. The couch was blocking a door I hadn't noticed until now.

Anna Kristine felt my stare. She looked at me and smiled wanly, and for a moment, I wanted to tell her everything. I wanted to cling to her and tell her that sitting in front of the TV with her reminded me of watching *Some Like It Hot* with Dad every Christmas. His choice. I wanted to tell her how his laugh sounded like someone gurgling, how recently he had died. My father was dead. Not my real father, but Dad. I felt a surge of forgiveness toward him.

I wanted to tell her about my mother, about my biological father, about how I had never wanted children but now, suddenly, knowing that I was pregnant, I couldn't imagine not having a child. I wanted, I wanted, I wanted. I wanted so much that what I wanted most was not to want. I wanted to talk and talk until there was nothing left to tell.

16.

Anna Kristine went to bed early, turning out the lights as she passed through the hall. It was only ten. I ripped a page out of a blank notebook and searched for a good pen. When I found the right one, I knelt down on the floor in front of the coffee table and started to write a letter to my child. It seemed the thing normal people would do.

"I wanted you to know how happy I was today, the day I found out about you," I wrote. My hand was shaking. "Being happy reminds you of all the times you haven't been." I read over what I'd written. Disgusting. I ripped the letter into shreds. I would not be the kind of mother who tells her child too much.

17.

Henrik had said I could use the phone to call my family. I considered calling Pankaj. *There must be someone else.* I should want to call Pankaj, I told myself, but I couldn't make myself dial his number. Our number. *There must be someone I'm closer to.*

A telephone book for Finnmark, its cover ripped off, sat by the phone. I began flipping through it, at first, absentmindedly;

then I looked for names. I searched for any Blixes that might live in Finnmark, and found none.

I skimmed through the listings in Masi and the nearby town of Kautokeino, where my mother had stayed. Any of the names could be my father's. I imagined my body might spasm in recognition and revolt when I saw his name. It was in my blood, I would know. But as I searched blindly, I grew more frantic. I had nothing to go on. He could be anyone. Everyone.

Empty Chair,
Hanging from Tree

1.

I knew the difference between knocks: Anna Kristine patted on my door with the flats of her fingers; Henrik rapped with his knuckles. The two of them were forever entering and exiting my room.

Henrik was at the door. It was late morning.

"You're looking better," he said, before really looking at me.

"I feel better, much better," I said.

I considered returning the compliment, but could think of nothing to say. His blond hair looked brighter today, like a halo. He was holding a magazine.

"What's that?" I said.

"Just came in the mail," he said. He handed it to me, and I studied the cover. A man holding a reindeer's face, turning it toward the camera. The reindeer was trying to turn away. The magazine was called *Reindriftsngtt Boazodoallo-Oddasat*.

"Magazine for reindeer herders," Henrik said.

I studied a picture of reindeer being tracked by satellite. Another photo showed protesters outside a London restaurant, carrying signs. SAVE RUDOLPH, they said.

"The Sami language looks complicated," I said.

"It's not complicated for us," Henrik said. He was chewing on a toothpick.

I handed the magazine back to him. "I thought I saw a little girl in my room yesterday. I didn't know if she was real." I tried to laugh.

"My niece. My sister was visiting from Oslo with her daughter. We didn't know where she had gone, and then we see that your door was open this much"—he showed a small distance between his large hands—"and then we knew."

"I've only seen you and Anna Kristine for the past few days. I started to forget there were other people here. Or anywhere."

"Sometimes I feel that way when I go out to see my reindeer. I go out there for days, and when I get back I forget how to talk to people." Henrik paused. "I'm going to check on them this afternoon."

"Can I go with you?" I asked.

"It's a long way. I think my aunt might get upset with me. I will check and see what Nature says."

Henrik pulled back one of the curtains. "Nature, do you think I can take this sick woman out into the cold?"

He cupped his ear and listened. He nodded as though taking in unsurprising information.

"But Nature," he said in a pleading voice, "are you sure? She's never seen a reindeer herd before."

Again he listened and nodded.

Finally, he turned to me. "I'm sorry," he said. "It's not going to happen today. Maybe when you get full recovery."

"I need to get out of here," I said. The desperation in my voice surprised both of us.

"I can understand," Henrik said. "But Anna Kristine wants you to stay in Kautokeino for another day so she can make sure you're healed."

"That's fine," I said. "I just need to get out of this room." If my mother's rapist had never been arrested, it was likely he still lived in town. I wasn't expecting to cry. I didn't want to cry. "I'm wondering if you can show me around. I just need to see ... something different." *I need to find him.*

"Okay," Henrik said. "Why don't you come to the bar tonight with me and my friends. Everyone in the town will be there."

I thanked him.

After he was gone, I saw he had left a handful of toothpicks on the bedside table.

2.

It was eleven p.m. by the time Henrik came to pick me up. I had been waiting for hours.

"Shhh! Anna Kristine is sleeping," I said before he said anything.

Henrik was with his cousin Isak. Isak had the body of a fourteen-year-old. It appeared he dyed his hair, too, but his was black. I could smell the alcohol on them. It didn't emanate from their breath as much as their necks.

I grabbed my hat and scarf. "Where have you been?" I said.

"Drinking at a friend's house," Isak said.

"It's too expensive to drink at bars here. Everyone drinks at home first," Henrik said, and added: "You're mad."

"I have no reason to be mad," I said.

"Don't be mad," Isak said. "We're just on Sami time here. Everyone's on Sami time. The sun is on Sami time."

We crossed the street and walked up a hill. My calves were instantly sore—they hadn't done anything for days. As we approached the bar, I heard laughter, both tinny and low. Through the windows of parked cars, I could see women and men overcrowded into backseats, bottles of wine and beer.

The first room of the bar had a dartboard and a large stage for karaoke. Two women who looked retarded were sitting by a speaker. Jeremy had never been to a bar. Or a party. The biggest event he'd ever attended was Dad's funeral. In many ways, I had failed him.

Back-to-back booths lined one long wall of the next room; a bar ran along the other. The bartender was wearing a shirt with a picture of a baby on it. Real stud earrings protruded through the shirt—one through each of the baby's ears and another through its belly button.

Henrik asked what I wanted to drink. I told him water, and he rolled his eyes. While he waited in line at the bar, Isak and I sat down at a booth. A man wearing a bright green sweatshirt introduced himself. He said his name twice, and when he repeated it a third time, I pretended I finally understood. The man, who looked about forty-five, was a school-bus driver. *Twenty-nine years ago he would have been sixteen. Too young.*

I asked him how far his route took him, and he told me the names of towns I had no reason to know.

He wanted to go to America, to Los Angeles. Did I think he could find work?

"Ignore him," said another man, Per Anders. He invited me to watch his reindeer be taken to the slaughterhouse. "Just the old ones we killing now, this time of year," he explained. "When they maybe fifteen she start to fall down, and her teeth come out."

He was tall, and I looked nothing like him. I declined.

More people were arriving. I studied the middle-aged men with darker coloring. I resembled none of them. I resembled all of them.

Henrik came to the table with drinks and a female companion. "This is my cousin Karin," he said. Karin had round eyes, black as pebbles. They both sat down.

"Hi," I said. "I was wondering where all the women were."

"There aren't many women our age here," she said. "The men become reindeer herders, or they work on the oil rigs over by Tromsø. But most of the women who grow up here go to Oslo. For college. They don't stay in the family business, because it's not women's business. Like my sister. She lives in Oslo now." She pointed to Oslo on the map of Norway imprinted on the beer glass. "Big Sami community there."

"Do they stand out down there?" I asked, and then tried to explain myself. "Does everyone know right away that they're Sami?"

Karin and Henrik looked at each other as though making sure they had the same answer. They shook their heads and turned back to me.

"Many Sami look like us," Henrik said, putting his arm around Karin. "But others can be like him." Henrik lifted his chin toward a tall man at the bar with blond hair and pinkish skin.

"You agree he could be surfer in California?" Karin said.

I nodded.

"Many people can't tell who's Sami," Henrik said. "We can tell, but ..." He took a sip of beer and didn't finish his sentence.

Someone turned up the volume on the bar's TV. A cross-country ski race in Switzerland. A skier from Kautokeino was in third place.

Cheers erupted in the bar, more eyes turned to the TV.

"You know why the Sami are such good skiers?" Karin asked. "Because their legs are like this." She stood up and, in her dress, exaggerated a bowlegged stance. It was exactly what Kari had demonstrated for me in Helsinki. "There was a study done some years ago, you know. They showed that Sami didn't get enough D vitamin. Their muscles grow, but not their bone. It's not so common anymore, but everyone, they used to be like that."

I looked around the room at the older men. My father would have a bowlegged walk.

3.

Henrik stood by the bar, his arm around a man wearing suspenders to hold up his ski pants.

"That's the mayor," Karin said.

"Really?" I said. He was a small man in his fifties, with ears that cupped forward. "How long has he been mayor?"

"Forever," Karin said.

I could become friendly with him and go see him at his office the next day—he would be able to help me. Henrik caught me looking at them. He steered the mayor over to the table, and they sat down. The mayor introduced himself. "I'm the mayor," he said, slurring. His handshake was damp, limp. "Do you want to hear a *yoik*?" he said.

"A joke?" I said.

He nodded.

"Sure," I said.

The mayor began yodeling. The song lasted a minute. Henrik, Karin, and a couple others clapped or cheered. The mayor took a swig of his beer.

I looked at Karin.

"That was a *yoik*," she said, pronouncing it *yolk*. "It's like a chant. Everyone has their own *yoik* that's particular to them. It's like, how do I explain? It's like a man and his shadow."

"What do people *yoik* about?"

"Something special that happened to them or something that characterizes them. The mayor's *yoik* is about his walk. He walks like a small bear."

I turned to the mayor. "Thank you," I said. "That was lovely."

"Where are you from?" he said. He was more drunk than I'd realized. He was struggling to keep his chin from his throat.

"New York," I said.

"Where are you from?" he said, this time addressing my chest.

"I'm going to go soon," I said to Henrik and Karin. I didn't know what I was doing in this bar. Dad was dead, my mother had been raped, and the mayor was talking to my breasts. "I need to go."

"I can take you," Karin said. "I have my car."

"Don't go," Henrik said. He reached across the table for my hand. He dropped it after a minute and argued with the mayor about who would buy the next round of drinks. They both brought out their wallets and placed them on the table, like poker chips. Seeing men's wallets made me sad. They were either too thick or too thin, too old or too new. They always looked wrong.

Karin and I made our way out of the bar. A man grabbed her elbow and said something that amused her. Her big teeth looked bigger when she laughed.

We stepped outside. The cold grabbed my nose, pinching it. I asked Karin where I could find out more about the Sami involved in the Alta Dam protests.

"Go to the Sami Parliament," she said, unlocking her car. "It's in Karasjok, not so far from here. They have recordings of everything."

"I passed through Karasjok," I said, more to myself than to her.

It was colder in Karin's car than it was outside. She apologized and blew onto the palms of her gloves. I didn't see how that could help.

"I am happy you're staying with Anna Kristine," she said. "So she don't get lonely. She is very lonely, I think. Her husband, he was buried ten years ago. And her daughter is gone. She marry a man in Spain."

I nodded.

"And her son, something was wrong with him." She touched her forehead and looked over at me.

"I didn't know she had a son."

"It was very sad," Karin said. "I think it broke her heart."

We turned onto the road to Anna Kristine's house.

"My brother was born with Down's syndrome," I said. "I don't know what you call that here."

Karin shrugged.

We pulled up in front of the house, and I thanked Karin for the ride.

"Maybe you don't tell Anna Kristine what I told you about her son."

"I can't talk to her anyway," I said.

4.

I rose early. Anna Kristine was already dressed, as usual, in her full Sami outfit. Her hair, which looked white when she wore it down, was now pinned up and gray. Ornate bronze clips replaced the bobby pins she usually used to secure her hat.

For breakfast, we ate hard-boiled eggs and toast with butter and thin strips of white-yellow cheese. At ten thirty, Anna Kristine left the house, and I dressed to go to Karasjok, to the Sami Parliament, to find records of the protesters from Kautokeino, of any arrests that were made. That would give me a list of names to start with. I could go down the list, knocking on doors. I would know him when I saw him.

There was a bus to Karasjok that afternoon, but I didn't want to wait. I was tired of buses, of the poisonous meditations they provoked. I stood on the side of the road, my thumb extended. It was colder today, the wind stronger. I wrapped my scarf up around my nose and pulled my hat down.

The first car didn't stop; the second did. The man was blond and wore a leather jacket over his Sami outfit. The woman had a higher hairline than I'd ever seen on anyone. I tried not to stare.

They didn't speak English, but they understood "Karasjok" and "Sami Parliament." They nodded yes, they were going that way, as though there was no other place they could be going.

Outside the window, all was white. Flat, snow-covered fields. In the distance, I saw a large shape hanging from a tree. A white plastic chair. The woman with the high hairline pointed at it, and she, her husband, and I laughed together for longer than we needed to.

5.

It took an hour and a half to drive from Kautokeino to Karasjok. The Sami Parliament was an enormous structure, half of it shaped like a teepee. It looked new, costly. We turned into the empty parking lot. The man and the woman said something to each other, and then to me. I ran to check. It was closed—today was Sunday. Anna Kristine had looked different today because she had been dressed for church.

The Sami couple asked where I'd like to go next, and I said the town center. Somehow they understood this and drove down a hill to a shopping area. Though the cars in the parking lot were empty, plumes of exhaust, veined with lavender, rose from their trunks. The cars had been left running while their drivers shopped.

The couple stepped out of the car, and I did, too. I shook their hands to thank them, and signaled that I was okay. They walked into the grocery store, and I was left in the parking lot, among the running cars.

I could get into any one of the cars and take off. I would drive a Ford, I decided, nothing obvious. I walked up to the window of a red one. The keys were in the ignition, the door unlocked. Discreetly, I looked around. No one was watching me. The lot was empty of people, all herded inside by the cold.

I would get in the car, pick up Henrik, and we would drive to his island in the west. Or to Russia. Together, he and I would raise this child.

6.

I walked out of the parking lot, away from bad ideas. I saw a sign for a Sami museum and followed the arrows up a long hill. Once I was inside the entrance, my palms fell onto my knees. I heard panting.

I was panting.

I paid the admission price. I was the only visitor. The museum was simple, plain—a sharp contrast to the Sami Parliament. One room displayed Sami outfits from various regions. I recognized the ones from Inari, from Kautokeino.

A map of the stars, a full wall, illustrated how the ancient Sami had relied on the sky to navigate. Lines connected the Samis' constellations. A skier, a reindeer, six stars for horns. I stood squinting at the galaxy of stars, making out shapes, until the museum closed.

7.

I hitched back to Kautokeino.

My ride was Sara, pronounced *Sorra*. She was an older woman, plump. She asked what I was doing in Finnmark. I told her I was researching the Alta Dam protests.

"That was an interesting time," she said.

"You were here?" I said.

"No, I was born here but didn't live here then." At a young age, she was sent south to a Norwegian school, as were most of the Sami in Finnmark at that time. "The government wanted the children to learn Norwegian, so we were sent to schools where we slept and lived."

"Boarding schools?" I said.

"Yes, boarding schools," she said. She looked out the window on my side, as if she'd just seen one. "They don't exist now. But the Alta Dam ... I was so taken from my heritage that I was embarrassed when I saw the protesters."

"Embarrassed?"

She nodded. "They chained themselves together, at their ankles," she said, and pointed to her wrists, "and I thought, *Why are they doing this? Everyone thinks we Sami are wild beasts, and now they are showing this is true.* So yes, I was embarrassed. Shameful. But now I see I was wrong. It was important, the protests. I was thinking like the worst Norwegians. Not like Sami. I had been brainwashed. Not really, of course. But how much my mind was changed. How much my thinking was changed."

Sara now worked for an organization that helped the Sami sustain their villages by manufacturing Sami handicrafts and exporting reindeer meat.

"How many Sami are there now?" I asked.

"The government says about fifty thousand to seventy thousand in all of Lapland. But I think that's wrong. I think it's closer to two hundred thousand," she said. "They tried to do a ... what's the word? Not a lottery." She rubbed her eyebrows. "Like when Joseph and Mary were going to Bethlehem, they were going there to do what?"

"A census?"

"Census," she said. "Yes, they try to do census, but many Sami didn't want to be part of it. Many Sami didn't want to be counted. They don't think they are Sami, or they do, but to them, they don't want to have to be a number."

"But you think they should be counted?"

"Yes," she said. "I do. It helps them get supports from the government. The government know nothing. They come up here and use our nature, our trees and oil and they treat us like we are nothing. Like we are sheep. 'Move over, sheep!' they say..." She trailed off. "And the Alta Dam disaster! They tried to sell the idea to the Sami by saying it would produce so many jobs. 'So many jobs it will produce. Hundred jobs. More,' they say. It created three jobs. Three! Those jobs were far away, in Narvik!"

The light in the sky around us was being squeezed out, like water from a rag. The song on her radio was the one about driving home for Christmas.

Sara turned to me then, as though she hadn't taken note of me before. "You look like someone," she said. "Have you been here before?"

"No," I said.

"You look like someone," she repeated. "Let me think who."

She was going to tell me I looked like a man she knew. Within the next minute, I would learn the identity of my father.

"Yes," Sara said and slapped her thigh. "I know who she is you look like."

I exhaled. It was a woman. She was going to tell me I looked like a woman on an American sitcom. People often told me I looked like her.

"She lives outside Alta, this woman you look like. She is American, I think from California. She works at the Ice Hotel in Alta."

"She works there now?"

"I saw her there a year ago. Maybe. Maybe nine months. For my job, I travel all over Finnmark, I meet everyone."

"She looks like me?"

"She's much older, but there is something similar. Or... maybe you are both American, that's all."

With fumbling fingers, I unzipped my backpack and took out the envelope with Eero's pictures of my mother. I removed the photo that I liked the best, the one that looked least how I remembered her, and held it in front of the steering wheel. Perhaps by choosing this one, I was ensuring it was less likely it would be her that Sara recognized. She took her eyes off the road to study it.

"Is it an old photo?"

"Yes," I said. "From maybe thirty years ago."

"Then maybe it's her," Sara said. "It's possible."

"Do you know her name?" I asked.

"What is it?" she said. "I'm trying think." She tapped the side of her head.

I was mouthing the word when she said it herself.

"Olivia."

Tongue to Ice

1.

My mother had returned to Lapland. She hadn't returned to her sisters in California. Or to New York, to us.

We had a funeral for you.

We approached Kautokeino. Sara asked where I was staying. I mumbled Anna Kristine's name, pointed to a road.

"Anna Kristine's famous around here," Sara said.

Sara wanted to come inside to say hello to Anna Kristine. I claimed she wasn't home, which turned out to be true.

I lay on the living-room couch, planning. I had been so certain when I had gone to San Antonio. I had held the address to Mr. Wells's house in my hands as if it were an engraved invitation. A decade had passed. I was still chasing her.

I called the Ice Hotel. "You are lucky," said the woman who answered the phone. "By mistake they built two extra rooms this year." She had a heavy accent; she was not my mother. I made a reservation for the following night.

Henrik came over that afternoon. He wore a plastic lasso around his neck, wrapped a dozen times.

"You missed a great after-party," he said, collapsing on the chair in my room. "What are you doing?"

"Looking at a map. I want to go to Alta, to the Ice Hotel tomorrow."

"I can take you," he said. "It's on the way to Tromsø. I was going to go to visit a friend who's working on an oil rig there. He's having a party this weekend. You can come."

"I'm not in the mood for a party," I said, measuring distances on the map with my fingers. I told him I was looking for my mother. That I didn't want to be alone when I saw her. "Would you want to—"

"I'll come with you," he said. He didn't ask what my mother might be doing in Lapland or why I thought she might be at the Ice Hotel.

"Great," I said. And then I said it again—this time, with enthusiasm. "Great."

2.

Anna Kristine insisted that I not pack up completely. She wanted to ensure I'd come back through Kautokeino, that she'd see me again. I picked out the clothes I would need and said good-bye to Anna Kristine. Pointing to a calendar, I showed her when I would return. She took my hand in hers and patted it three times—once for each day.

Henrik asked me to drive Anna Kristine's car. He'd been out until four, and had to wake up at seven to herd his reindeer. I let the car warm up for five minutes—not long enough. I had to drive with my gloves on. I sat on my left foot to keep it warm.

As we passed by Masi, Henrik stared at the river. His mouth

was open, as though he wanted to say something. I fixed my gaze on the road ahead. Five kilometers later, when I dared to look at him, Henrik was asleep. He slept sitting straight up. Pankaj could never fall asleep in the car.

3.

The Ice Hotel was constructed entirely of snow and ice. It looked like an architect's version of a child's dream fort. A permanent structure made of wood had been built next to the ice structure. Reception.

Six women stood behind the reception desk. All were young, and none was my mother. A relief—I wasn't ready to see her. Twenty tourists, many of them Asian, waited in line.

A woman named Mariann checked us in. Tonight, she told us, was the official opening. Given the late snowfall this year, they hadn't been able to start constructing the hotel as early as scheduled. There wasn't enough snow to build the structure, and it hadn't been as cold as necessary to keep the hotel from melting. "Artists from around the planet—they have just been sitting around waiting," Mariann said as she handed me a registration card.

The card asked for my address. My father's house in Rhinebeck, the apartment I shared with Pankaj in Morningside Heights—neither seemed like home. When I pictured their interiors, their shapes were *Room at Arles* slanted, the walls collapsing. I asked Henrik for Anna Kristine's address and scribbled it on the blank line.

4.

We were instructed to go to the activity center, two rooms over in the wood building, to get outfitted for our stay. It resembled a ski store, with tall shelves of boots stocked in one room; in the other, snowsuits hung according to size. They still held the shapes of previous users—shoulders, knees, elbows.

I chose a small blue suit; Henrik picked out a red one, a men's medium. We were fitted for boots, gloves, hats. An entire uniform was necessary to find my mother.

I studied every female employee. My mother had blond hair when I last saw her, but fourteen years had passed. A brunette across the room was wearing suede pants, a black sweater. I moved closer. She was speaking German. *Look at the ears*, I told myself. *Just look at the ears.*

5.

Henrik and I dragged our suits and boots and luggage to the lockers. A troll-like woman gave us a key. All around us, men, women, and children stripped down to their long underwear— light blues and pinks and faded reds, the colors of laundry mistakes. I took my snowsuit into the women's restroom. I've never changed in public.

I returned to the luggage room and stood watching Henrik from six feet away. He saw my stare. "What?" he said.

"Nothing," I said. When you believe anyone could be your mother, you begin to think anyone could be your brother, your lover, your son.

6.

We tried to enter the Ice Hotel, but we were stopped a few feet in by a woman with a shovel. She said something to Henrik. "It's not done yet," he translated for me. "Let's go for a walk until six. That's when the party starts."

With flashlights, we walked down the road. We watched a school bus stop, kids file out.

When we tired of walking, we lay down side by side on a clearing just beyond the road, staring upward.

"Can I ask you something?" he said.

"You don't have to," I said, and I told him about my mother.

When I was finished, he reached his hand out toward mine but didn't touch it. "Are you sure you want to do this?" he said.

I nodded at the dark sky.

7.

At six, a man in a reindeer-skin poncho sounded an animal horn. The doors to the Ice Hotel opened, and everyone filed in, two by two. A chandelier, its tears made of ice, hung from the ceiling of packed snow. Sculptures of Norse gods, like glass statues, lined the main hallway.

"I didn't know it would be this beautiful," Henrik said.

I nodded absently. Where was she?

We were led to a large room at the end of the hallway: the Ice Bar. A sheer block of ice spanned the length of the room, thirty feet. A sculpture of a harp stood in one corner. We made our way to the bar. No mother. Instead, five bartenders, all women, who needed to read the menu to make the drinks. "First night," they said.

Henrik ordered the house specialty, and I ordered water. The drinks were served in square ice glasses. Henrik toasted my glass with his. I moved to the center of the room, and Henrik followed. Everyone had changed into outfits more appropriate for a club than an igloo—leather pants and boots, suede or wool ponchos. Henrik and I were the only guests still wearing our snowsuits.

In the corner, two employees were putting the finishing touches on the room. A woman was running a clothing iron over the edges of an ice bench, smoothing the surface. The iron was plugged into a long extension cord.

"After all that time I spent ironing your dress, I wish you wouldn't wear your seat belt," my mother once said to me. I had been on my way to a school formal.

Henrik stepped back and looked down. A little girl had run into his legs and was now sitting on the snow-covered ground, staring up at us.

Her parents approached, and the mother said something to Henrik.

Henrik translated for me: "New boots."

The man was from the West Indies, a glassblower. He and his wife had a store down the road from the hotel, and invited us to stop by. They and other local artists constructed the rooms of the hotel by inflating enormous parachute balloons and packing the outsides of the balloons with snow. When each room had its shape, they deflated the balloons. "Like papier-mâché," said the woman.

We were gathered around the girl as though she were a fire. The woman picked up her daughter—she had bright blue eyes and cornrowed hair. Eva.

"You watch out, you two," the mother said. "This baby has inspired more babies than you could imagine."

I looked at Henrik and saw that he was about to speak, to correct her. But when he opened his mouth, he said, "I can see why." He stroked the side of Eva's face with the back of his gloved hand.

8.

Henrik asked the couple if they knew a woman named Olivia, who worked at the hotel. They looked at each other and shook their heads no.

My mother wasn't the kind of person you forgot once you had met her. "Everyone loves your mother until they stop," Dad once said. It was one of the few times I saw him drunk. My mother had been making him martinis all night.

I now had little to say to the couple. There were other people to ask.

"Well, it was nice talking to you," I said, and backed away.

"That was rude," Henrik said, after he excused himself from their conversation and caught up with me.

"I have no time to be nice," I said. "I don't think you understand."

"Relax," he said. "Please, relax."

"I can't," I said.

"It's time for dinner anyway," Henrik said. "Come. She might be a cook. It is possible."

"No, it's not possible." Dad had done all the cooking.

The restaurant was in the same building as reception. Henrik and I were seated at a small table near a window and a heater. We unzipped and removed the tops of our snowsuits, the sleeves hanging by our feet like tired skins. A red ornament in the shape of a snowflake dangled in front of the window. Henrik spun it.

Our waitress was not my mother. The chef was a man. "She probably doesn't work here anymore," I said to Henrik. "She never stayed in one place for very long anyway. I'm such a fool."

Henrik did not argue.

9.

After dinner, we had two options: retire to our ice beds or return to the bar.

The bar crowd had thinned, and conversations between strangers were expected, encouraged by drink. Three Dutchmen were sticking their tongues to the ice bar while their friend took a picture.

Two of the female bartenders—one with a fake tan and the other looking sickly in comparison—bounded onstage. "We are singing songs we hope you like!" said one. The first song they sang was "Mamma Mia." They had choreographed their dances, but it was clear by the next song, "Mustang Sally," that they only had a limited number of moves.

"Are they on a horse or a motorcycle?" I asked Henrik.

"I think they're in a car," he said. "A Mustang."

The girl in the passenger seat was miming rolling down her window. The woman in the driver's seat was cupping her breasts.

"Shouldn't she be keeping her hands on the wheel?" I asked.

I was impatient for the night to be over, for it to be morning, so we could leave.

"Look at my glass," Henrik said. He was on his third refill. On the side, where his lips had warmed it, the glass was as thin as paper. The women, finished with their set, circled around, collecting melting glasses in a bucket.

"Do I get a new one for free?" Henrik asked the woman who had been driving the Mustang.

She shook her head no.

"I'll get you another one," I offered. The woman's braids, her tan, depressed me.

At the bar, I ordered a drink for Henrik. "Go light on the vodka," I instructed the bartender, who looked nineteen. I didn't want to spend the night in an ice room with a drunken man.

When I returned to Henrik, he stared at me.

"I think I found her," he said.

"What?" I turned to look behind me.

"I can't be sure, but ..."

"I don't care. Just tell me."

"The singing woman knows Olivia."

I watched his lips after they had stopped moving, to see if I had misunderstood. "What? How?"

"She says a woman named Olivia runs the wilderness trips."

"Wilderness trips," I repeated, trying to make sense of the words.

"We can sign up tomorrow morning."

I was still holding his drink. I extended my hand and gave it to him. "Henrik," I said, and then said nothing.

10.

In the locker room, we prepared for bed. Henrik opened the locker, handed me my clothes. I couldn't speak. I tried to pay attention as the troll woman cautioned us to not dress too warmly. Extra layers could make you sweat in the night, then freeze, she explained. The troll handed us each a cotton sheet to wrap around our bodies. I didn't understand why, but I took one.

Henrik and I sprinted through the hotel in our long underwear and boots. *Why didn't anyone tell me how bad those culottes looked on me?* Our room was in the back, the farthest from the entrance. I parted the curtain and ducked through the arched doorway. A large block of ice, covered with reindeer skin, stood in the middle of the room. Lights ran around the edges of the bed, illuminating it, like a game show.

I laid out my sleeping bag on the right side of the bed—with Pankaj, I slept on the left. I secured my hat and tightened its ties around my chin. I clicked off the light switch and pulled the hood of the sleeping bag up over my head.

"Are you awake?" I said to Henrik.

He didn't answer.

"Are you awake?" I said again, a little louder, to wake him if he was on the cusp.

Nothing.

Inside my sleeping bag, I took off my gloves and placed my fingers on my stomach. I could feel something deeper than hunger.

11.

I woke up at five in the morning. I had to pee. I slipped out of my sleeping bag and into my boots and sprinted through the corridors of the hotel. Beneath my feet, the ice sounded like twigs snapping. The cold speared at my shins.

I made my way to the bathroom—it was in the main building—and then to the shower room. I was alone. I undressed, turned on all five shower heads, sat on the floor, and closed my eyes. I turned toward one of the streams of water and felt it thrum against my forehead.

The truth about my relationship with Pankaj: twice, when he told me he loved me, I pretended to be asleep.

12.

I was waiting outside the door to the activity center when it opened at eight a.m. I told an employee named Helga I was curious about the wilderness trip.

"Yes, you take snowmobile out to cabin and there you have huskies and dinner and warm fire. And tomorrow you take snowmobile back."

"Who's at the cabin?"

"The woman who takes care of the cabin."

"What's her name?" I asked.

"Liv is her name, I think."

"Olivia?"

"Yes, Livia."

I said I'd like to sign up for the trip, that night.

Helga waited for her computer to boot up. She squinted at

the screen. "There are two couples going. Swedish it looks like. And Japanese. How many for you?"

"There are two of us."

She quoted me a price in kroner. I did the math. Fifteen hundred dollars.

"Only one then," I said.

Point Zero

1.

I returned to the ice room. Henrik was sitting up in his sleeping bag, drinking something red.

"Lingonberry juice," he said. His hat was perched sideways on his head, making him look like a child in need of care. "A woman came this morning, carrying a tray. Where were you?"

"I couldn't sleep after five. I got up, took a shower, had breakfast, asked about the wilderness trip." I told him the cost, and he swore in Sami. "That's ridiculous," he said.

"I'll stay at my friend's house in Alta," he offered. "You'll be okay?"

I told him I would be fine from here on out.

"What's *herehonhout*?"

"From now until the future."

"And when we get to the future you will fall apart?"

2.

The trip didn't leave until late that afternoon. We decided to spend the day at the Alta Dam. Henrik made a call and discovered we needed a tour guide, someone who had access to the gates and to the tunnel that led to the dam itself.

Our guide, Günter, was German. We met him at a gas station—the only clear landmark he could think of—and stepped out of the car to introduce ourselves. Günter moved to Alta when his Norwegian girlfriend got a job at the local museum. I stared at the underside of his nose as he spoke. It was a large nose, and he was tall and swayed backward when standing.

Henrik moved to the backseat of the car; Günter ducked as he got into the passenger seat, and directed me to the dam. We drove past an abandoned checkpoint known as Point Zero. "This is where they began building the road to the dam," Günter said. "Before this, there was no road out there. Here at Point Zero is where all the Sami would protest, yes?" he said, looking at Henrik. "Where they would chain themselves together. There were a thousand of them. They had to ship in policemen from the south. There are some funniest stories from that time actually. For example, there was a bus company the policemen would hire to take the demonstrants from Point Zero back to Alta, but then the company would pick up more demonstrants in Alta and bring them back to the protest. They were being paid both ways, yes?"

"It's *demonstrators*," I said. "Not *demonstrants*."

Günter paused, stared at me, and continued. He told us the controversy over the dam divided many families. But there were also stories of policemen and protesters falling in love. They were still married and lived in Alta, he said.

We approached another bridge. "This is a famous bridge," Günter continued, "because some of the Sami protesters tried to blow it up. But they didn't know what they were doing, so one of the men blew off his arm. He had to leave Norway for many years afterwards. It is said that he is the only terrorist in Norwegian history."

"Not the only one," Henrik said quietly. "Just more famous."

I turned to look at him briefly over my shoulder.

"A few days after that my cousin tried a similar intervention. But he didn't even get to the bridge. He lost his hand and an eye."

"Really?" I said. "Isak's brother?"

"No, another cousin. Older. Anna Kristine's son."

"Where is he now?" Karin had told me that he wasn't right in the head, and I had assumed he lived in a home, like Jeremy.

"He's been at an insane asylum in Tromsø for years."

I glanced at Henrik in the rearview mirror.

"Anna Kristine says she knew the day he was born that something wasn't right with him," Henrik said, averting his eyes from mine. He stared out the window, peering down as we crossed the bridge.

3.

We approached a small mountain with a gate at its base. Günter punched in a code, and the gate unlocked and lifted. We drove inside the tunnel and registered our names and nationalities. "In case something happens they'll know how many people to search for," Günter explained. I studied the registration book;

we were the first visitors to the dam in over a week. We parked the car. The tunnel had a paved road, but the walls looked like those of a cave. Water dripped and echoed.

We walked with flashlights toward a door. OBSERVATION DECK THIS WAY, read a sign. Günter pushed on the door, but it didn't open. He tried shouldering it. "Frozen," he said.

"I have some matches," Henrik offered. He lit a match, and the breeze blew it out. He tried again. He held the lit match close to the lock on the door, and the snow started to melt. Three more matches, and the door could be opened.

Wind churned into the tunnel. We stepped outside, pulling up our hoods. Günter propped the door open with his scarf, to ensure we wouldn't get locked out. We walked to the center of the observation deck. The dam was three hundred feet wide, and the deck spanned the length of it. Water channeled through the pipes beneath us—the sounds of an untuned organ.

I stared out into the distance, at the easy turns the river took.

What kind of woman leaves her family to live above the Arctic Circle?

Then again: *What kind of woman pretends to be asleep when her fiancé tells her he loves her?*

4.

We dropped Günter off at the gas station, and Henrik drove us back to the hotel. I said good-bye to him and made a plan to meet him in the same place the next morning.

"Good luck," he said. He looked at me a moment too long.

I arrived at the activity center, dressed and packed for the trip, and was asked to wait for the others from the group to check in. Half an hour passed before a squat man approached me. He was wearing a ski hat with a rainbow-colored pompom on top.

"You go on wilderness adventure?" he asked. I nodded. His name was Olaf, and he would be my guide.

"Clarissa," I said, and shook his hand. He had hair on his knuckles.

"You are only one," Olaf said. "The others did not come."

I had hoped to hide behind them, to observe my mother unnoticed. "What if I change my mind and go tomorrow night?" I asked.

"You lose all money," he said.

"The woman named Olivia is at the hut?" I asked.

"Yes, she is there."

"And she stays there all night?"

"Yes. We go on scooter two hours. I leave and you sleep and I come in morning."

"Okay," I said.

Olaf asked how many layers I was wearing under my snow-suit. I pushed up the sleeve of my fleece pullover and showed him the archaeology of my attire: turtleneck, two layers of long-sleeved thermal underwear. He nodded in approval and asked about my legs. "Long underwear and jeans," I said.

He handed me a ski mask, and I fastened it over my face. I looked like I was preparing to rob the Bank of Lapland. I tightened the strap of my reindeer-skin hat below my chin and followed Olaf out into the cold. A dozen snowmobiles were parked in two lines, and Olaf stopped in front of them. Through the holes in his mask, I could see his small eyes.

"Is it safe?" I asked. I was thinking of the child growing inside me.

"Yes," he said, "is safe. Something is wrong?"

"I don't know," I said. "Should I be scared?"

"No," he said. "Are you scary?"

"I'm not scary, no."

"Don't be scary for me," he said.

Olaf backed up a snowmobile and gave me a lesson. He showed me how to start the engine and how to brake. He told me he would lead the way and would put up his hand when he wanted me to stop. He demonstrated. He looked like he was taking an oath.

The snowmobile was more difficult to steer and less steady than I expected. There were tracks, but I slipped to the right and to the left as we rode. We drove past an old cemetery, its tombstones like teeth. I ducked behind the windscreen to shelter my face, but my hands burned. I couldn't keep them on the handlebars. And Olaf was far ahead, winding through the forest. Above me, the moon was a comma in the sky, a conjunction between days.

5.

Olaf raised his hand to signal that I should slow down. We had been driving for an hour. I pulled up behind him. He walked toward me.

Now is when he kills me.

"Now is when I make a fire for you and we have hot lingon-berry juice," he said.

Olaf lifted three pieces of firewood out of a compartment on the back of his snowmobile. From a pouch attached to his belt, he pulled out a knife. He was still wearing his mask. I took a step back and sank into the snow. I had left my knife at Anna Kristine's house.

"Don't be scary," he said.

He used the knife to carve down the edges of the wood, the way scissors are used to curl a ribbon. When he was done, he had three sculptures of palm trees. He got out a match.

"It's like the Jack London story," I said.

"Are you from England?"

"No, America," I said. He looked confused. I stayed quiet.

We sat by the fire, the slender moon and the orange and aubergine flames our only light. He opened a thermos and poured me a cup of what he said was hot lingonberry juice. *It's a drug.* I pretended to sip.

I asked Olaf if he had children. I wanted to remind him that if he had daughters, he would best think of them now, before murdering me.

He did have daughters: Camilla and Anne Britt.

"I love Norwegian names," I said dumbly. What I meant was, *I love that you have daughters.*

"Yes, our food is very good," he said.

He drank two cups of lingonberry juice. Relieved that he'd drunk it and he had girls, I took a sip. The juice tasted sour, like unripened cherries. I could feel the liquid heat slip down my throat and chest before expanding outward.

Olaf asked if I had tried reindeer meat. I said I had.

"The Sami have reindeer," he said.

"Yes, the Sami are often compared to Native Americans," I said, trying to make conversation. *If I'm talking he can't kill me.* "Some Native Americans are nomadic. They follow buffalo, Sami follow reindeer."

Olaf nodded. "The Sami are like your ... what do you call them?"

"Native Americans?"

"Yes," he said, proud of his observation.

He turned his back to the fire and, like a dog, kicked snow onto the flames. I complained to him about my burned hands, and he showed me a switch on the handlebar. "Hand-warmer," he explained.

Olaf broke off a number of large sticks from nearby bushes and carried them in one hand, like a bouquet. "So we can find our way back," he said.

I nodded. I didn't understand.

The next part of the trip was easier. The fields were flat

and open and appeared glaucous in the dim moonlight. Olaf stopped occasionally to plant a stick in the snow.

After half an hour, we turned, and I saw a structure in the distance, a cabin. I slowed. Ahead of me, Olaf stopped and turned off his engine. Dogs let out high-pitched howls, the sound of strong wind.

The cabin's shutters were open, and a single lit candle stood in each window, winking.

I braked next to Olaf, and he turned off my engine for me. The dogs' howls grew so loud I covered my ears. Olaf sidestepped up to the entrance of the cabin—the hill was steep—and I trailed him by six feet. I wanted to see her before she recognized me.

The door opened. *"Velkommen,"* a man said. A man. All this way, and she wasn't here. My head fell forward in defeat.

"Are you okay?" I heard a voice say. My mother's. The same voice I often heard in my head. Now the voice was asking if I was okay. I stood up straight. I stepped to my left to get a better view.

It was her.

6.

I removed my face mask and walked closer. Her eyes were the blue of a stove's flame, brighter than I remembered them. Her hair was cut short and jagged, her straight blond bangs coming to points across her forehead—a crown inverted. Her figure was curvy but compact, stuffed into black motorcycle pants. On her left hand, she wore a strange glove.

The young man extended his hand. He had a long face and an impatient handshake. "Peter," he said. He was twenty years younger than my mother.

"Clarissa."

My mother stuck out her hand, without introducing herself.

"So here you are," she said, staring at my nose.

7.

She gave no further indication that she knew me. Peter welcomed us inside.

I stomped the snow from my shoes and removed them. Olaf unzipped and stepped out of his snowsuit, and I did the same. A fire was burning in the furnace, and we hung the suits from a hat stand close to the flames.

My mother offered us coffee. Olaf accepted; I declined. The skin around her mouth was smooth, her lips thin and parted. Wrinkles, like the dark, uneven edges of water stains, circled her eyes. Maybe tears had caused the damage. Nights spent crying with regret.

She disappeared into the kitchen, and I sat on a couch. Cheese and crackers had been arranged on a coffee table—too much of each. She had been expecting more people.

Peter and Olaf sat around the table, speaking Norwegian, laughing. I wanted to slap them, stuff the pompom from Olaf's hat into his mouth. They noticed my silence and switched to English.

"Do you live here, too?" I asked Peter. My voice sounded accusatory.

"No, nearby," he said. Olivia—he gestured toward the kitchen—worked for his tour business. They specialized in husky trips and overnight excursions to the hut.

I looked in the direction he was pointing. I had spent fifteen years waiting for this. My mother was stalling. She could be crawling out the window, running away. It hadn't occurred to me that she didn't want to be found. I had come to picture her as a ruined and lost woman, with bags packed, looking out the window, waiting for someone to take her home.

I was standing up to go look for her, when she came back into the living room, carrying coffee for Olaf. What I had thought was a glove was a splint on her thumb.

"What happens?" Olaf asked her, nodding at her hand. I sat back down.

"It was so stupid," she said, addressing her thumb. "I cut my thumb to the bone when I was chopping firewood last week. I have to wear this leather thing when I'm near the stove. The cut's sensitive to heat."

I tried to picture her thin arms chopping wood. My mother in her fifties, wearing motorcycle pants and wielding an axe. I wished Dad were alive, so I could tell him. *So absurd,* he would say. When he was troubled by something, he said it was *absurd. So absurd.*

"Are you sure you don't want something?" she asked, looking in my direction. With her good hand, she was tugging at the back of her hair.

"Maybe tea," I said. I didn't want her in the room until she was my mother again. Asking for tea would give her a chance to reenter, playing the right part.

She stared at me. Maybe she didn't recognize me. I stared back.

"You have to excuse me. I'm a little deaf in one ear. From the dogs barking."

"Tea," I said louder. Was she blind as well?

Olaf and Peter had slipped back into Norwegian. Fine. I glanced around the cabin. There was no electricity, only candlelight. Everything was old. The cracker plate was chipped, the candles were burned down to stubs. I neatened a stack of sled-dog magazines on the coffee table.

The dogs had stopped barking. It was now too quiet. I could hear my heartbeat; I could smell my snowsuit drying by the fire. The scent of damp money. I wanted Peter and Olaf to leave, so I could talk to my mother in private. I did the math. I had fourteen hours with her. If eight of them were spent asleep, we would still have six.

She came back with the tea for me, and sat down. Again, she played with the back of her hair. Gathering it and letting go, gathering it and letting go. Four of us were congregated around the table, two of us related but acting as though we had just met. I had recognized her right away, the way you know the key to your house on a ring of others. *Maybe she was in an accident. Amnesia.* I had never believed in dramatic scenarios people offered, but now they seemed likely.

"What kind of dogs are they?" I asked. "Siberian huskies?"

"No, Alaskan huskies. They're not as purebred as Siberian, but they're the best pulling dogs." My mother's voice was chirpy, deceptively inviting.

"How do the dogs get along?" I asked, looking at her.

She nodded before answering. "They're like a school class. They each have a personality. One's a troublemaker, another's a brat. It's very funny." She was fielding my questions the way she would those from any tourist. It was clear she was wholly uncurious about me.

"What time do you have to wake up?" I asked.

"In the summer I get up at nine." She held her teacup to her lips but didn't take a sip. "In the winter, five."

"Five," I repeated. Dad had consistently gotten us up for school while my mother had slept in. Five.

"Are the dogs like children?" I said, more pointedly than I'd wanted to.

She didn't take offense.

Again, she nodded before speaking. "When they're puppies, they're like children," she said. "But when they grow up, they're like partners. In fact, you can learn a lot from a good old lead dog."

I glanced around the room, at Peter and Olaf. They seemed to be following what she was saying. I suspected she had lost her mind. How could she be talking to me about children and partners?

"A lead dog," I repeated absently.

8.

"Would you like a sauna?" my mother asked. She rose suddenly. The room seemed thrown off balance, as though she had stood up in a small boat.

"Excuse me?"

"There's a sauna outside. I started it a few hours ago so it should be warm by now. Usually, the women go to the sauna hut first, then the men."

"Okay," I said.

Olaf and Peter were immersed in a conversation. Still laughing.

"Would you like a sauna beer?" my mother asked.

"What's that?"

"A beer you take in the sauna," she said.

I passed.

We stepped out of the cabin, and she led me to another, smaller cabin next to the outhouse. Inside the sauna cabin was a dressing room, with an assortment of chairs set out, as in a doctor's office. Steam had coated the mirrors. She told me how to adjust the temperature and instructed me on when to use the bucket of water.

"Aren't you going to take one, too?" I asked. We were standing in the changing room, its walls sweating.

"No, I can't go in there. The heat hurts my hand. I haven't had a sauna in weeks."

I stared at her. It was the first time I had been face-to-face with her, and so close. I had grown or she had shrunk: we were the same height.

"I have something to tell you," I said.

"Yes, I know," she said. "You're my daughter."

I nodded.

"I knew the second you walked in the door," she said. The corners of her mouth turned upward. I believed she might hug me.

"I knew this might happen one day." She extended her finger to the mirror and drew a vertical line. "I thought it was Richard who would track me down," she said, looking at the line. She traced a flower, transforming the line into a stem. "I don't have anything to say to him, and I don't have anything to say to you. If I had, I could have written you a letter."

"Don't you feel any obligation?" I said. I wanted to ask, *Any bit of love?* But I spared myself having to hear the answer.

"That was not my life. I had every reason to seek something else."

"But you had chosen that life," I said.

"No, decisions were made for me," she said. She held her forefinger in the air, as though scolding me. "I didn't make them."

I reached for her finger to slap it down, but before I could make contact, she returned her arm to her side.

"Why don't you take your sauna while I finish dinner," she said. She turned to leave. Her narrow back was facing me. I bolted forward to shove her, but she had already stepped out the door.

9.

I stripped out of my clothes. My pants snagged around my thick socks like shackles. I sat down on the floor and tugged them off with such force that the right pant-leg ripped. I had been sweating profusely while talking to my mother, and my clothes smelled musty. I kicked them into the corner and stepped into the sauna.

I sat naked, my back against the warm blond wood. My heart was a fist, and my lungs were full of heat. I was not the only child in the world who had been born of a rape. In some cultures, the mothers were disowned by their families. But the women didn't disown their children. That was the difference.

My mother's vagina was covered with blond-gray hairs. I used to watch her dress while hiding under her bed. Even then, the hair had been gray. I'd study the scar from her C-section.

That's where I came from, I'd say to myself. I wanted to know what she looked like naked now, to see what my body would look like at her age, after carrying a child. I wanted to know how close to death she was.

I sat in the sauna for half an hour. I pictured her face and tried to spit, but the heat had dried my tongue. I ran my fingers over my body—I hadn't thought of it in days. Lifting my legs, one at a time, I examined my thighs, my calves. I touched my stomach and imagined a small swell.

And then I recalled something I'd read once when I was researching Jeremy's condition. How overheating during pregnancy could cause birth defects. I ran out of the sauna and into the dressing room.

"Shit," I screamed to the room, to the steamed mirrors, to the chairs circled around me. The heat had gone to my head, affecting my balance. Pulling on my long underwear, I toppled. My hand broke my fall. Pain shot like static through my wrist and up my forearm.

"Shit, shit, shit."

10.

I sprinted out of the sauna hut. The cold paddled my face. Down below, past the cabin, the dogs barked crazily. It was clear how someone could be deafened by their cries.

Inside the cabin, Peter and Olaf were drinking beer. So much had happened, and they were sitting where I had left them. Olaf had taken off his hat, and I was surprised to see he was bald. He looked ancient, ugly without his hat, ridiculous as it was.

"Where's Olivia?" I asked. I was certain she was gone.

"She's feeding the dogs," Peter said.

"She say we stay for dinner," Olaf said.

"Of course," I said. *Of course she doesn't want to be alone with me.*

I stepped up to the living-room window to look out below. The dogs were chained to their individual dog huts, waiting for food. My mother, with a flashlight on her forehead, was slicing something, doling it into various bowls.

"What do they eat?" I asked, my back still turned to the men.

"Tonight, frozen salmon," Peter said.

"Who gets served first?" I watched my mother bypass a barking dog. "The lead dogs?"

"The dog that begs little," Peter said.

11.

My mother returned to the house, pounding her feet on the doormat. She liked to make an entrance. Once inside, she busied herself in the kitchen.

"Can I help?" I said.

"No, why don't you sit in the living room and relax," she said. She saw my offer for what it was—another attempt to be close to her.

"Taft's dead, by the way," I said.

"Who?" She was peeling a carrot.

"Taft. The cat that lived next door."

"Oh, that's too bad," she said. I watched her hand—she continued peeling the carrot without pause.

"I ran him over," I said.

"I need to concentrate on dinner," she said.

"Are you on drugs?" I said.

"You poor thing," she said. "You always tried so hard to get a reaction from me." She shook her head. "Can you put another log on the fire?"

12.

At dinner, I was seated across from her, but she avoided my stare. She winced as she removed her leather thumb-protector and placed it on her lap. On the table, she had set out salmon, bread, rice, and a small salad.

"Wine?" she offered, looking at the salmon.

Peter and Olaf said yes, and she brought out a box. The way she removed the nozzle from inside the box was pornographic. I couldn't watch.

"Did you like Ice Hotel?" Peter asked.

"It's fine," I said. "It's pretty, I guess." It seemed a year since I'd been there.

"Expensive," Olaf said.

"Sure," my mother said. "But we should be happy. The tourists there pay our bills."

She raised a glass, and Peter and Olaf clinked theirs against hers.

Olaf turned his glass toward me.

"I'm drinking water," I said. He took this as sufficient explanation.

"You don't want wine?" Peter asked. He was leaning back in his chair, playing the man of the house.

"No thanks," I said. "I'm pregnant." I hadn't planned on saying this, but suddenly I wanted my mother to know.

"Congratulations," Peter said.

"Yes, congratulations," my mother said.

"I miss what you say," Olaf said.

Peter said something to Olaf in Norwegian.

"Very good," Olaf said. He raised his glass toward me again. This time, I clinked mine against his to avoid having to avoid him.

"Who's the father?" my mother asked.

"My fiancé," I said. "Pankaj."

"Is he Indian?" she asked.

"He's Gita's son," I said.

"Oh," she said.

"She's doing fine," I said. "I'll tell her you said hello."

"I'm confused," Peter said.

"Any suggestions for mothering?" I said, ignoring Peter.

"No suggestions, really," my mother said. "People should act as they see fit."

Olaf asked her something in Norwegian, and she answered. My mother had learned Norwegian. Peter joined in, and soon they were speaking Norwegian for the rest of the conversation.

I couldn't avoid staring at my mother. At the way she occasionally looked down at her body to make sure she hadn't spilled anything on her snug black sweater. At the way she laughed too hard at the things Peter said.

Peter's face was red with drink. Maybe with love. With one hand, he held a wineglass; I couldn't see the other hand. I deliberately dropped my napkin and bent down to retrieve it. Under the table, I expected to see his hand on my mother's thigh, but it was hanging limply by the side of his chair.

At the end of dinner, the men helped clean up. Then they each steadied themselves with a hand on the wall as they put on their boots. My mother hugged them both good-bye. I had the impression that if Peter weren't there, if he weren't my mother's boss, she would have asked Olaf to take me back to the hotel that night.

"I come tomorrow at eight," Olaf said to me, and pointed to his wrist, where a watch would be if he were wearing one.

13.

"You can sleep in whichever one you want," my mother said, gesturing to the room of bunk beds. Each bed had a sleeping bag at its foot.

"Where do you usually sleep?" I asked.

"I'm going to sleep on the couch in the living room tonight," she said instead of answering my question. "I'm so tired I'll probably fall asleep right away. You can stay up with the lights on in that room."

I chose the bed that was the closest one to the doorless doorway between bunk room and living room.

My mother used the outhouse, paired the socks that had hung from the clothesline above the furnace, and washed her face and brushed her teeth in the kitchen sink. Between her thumb and forefinger, she extinguished every candle but the ones by my bed and the couch. I was sitting on the bottom bunk, watching her. She was wearing long underwear now, and I could make out her sharp nipples, the circles of fat that seemed to have settled above her thin knees.

"Good night," she said, as she lay down on the couch. If I strained my neck, I could see the lower half of her body. It was nine, too early to sleep. We both knew that. She blew out her candle.

"Richard died two weeks ago," I said into the darkness of the living room.

There was a long pause. "I'm sorry to hear that," she said.

A puddle of wax had formed at the base of the candle by my bed. I dipped my finger in the wax and waited for it to dry. I did this with each finger until all were coated. I clenched my fists and watched the wax crack.

14.

I woke to the sound of whimpers. Fumbling for matches, I lit a candle and carried it to the couch. My mother was sitting up, her head cradled in her hand. I knelt in front of her. She was crying, her fingertips pressed into her eyelids. The sleeping bag was gathered at her waist, so it appeared she was wriggling out of its cocoon. I made my way around the coffee table and sat next to her. She didn't look at me. I could hear her inhales, little gulps, her frequent swallows. I could smell her tooth-paste, something like licorice. I stayed near her, watching the profile of her face, her shiny cheek, the rip in her earlobe.

I moved closer. Our knees were touching.

"You have no idea what I've been through," she said, finally facing me. In the candlelight, her face was both frightened and haunting.

"Tell me," I said.

She turned her head, shifted her knees away from me. I put my hand on hers. "Ouch," she cried out. It was her left hand.

"I'm sorry," I said.

"Go back to bed or get out," she said.

I stood and lifted the candle to guide my way.

15.

In the morning, I woke to the sounds of springs sighing and my mother's socked feet hitting the floor. "Here we go again," she said to herself. I slithered out of my sleeping bag.

"I'm putting on coffee," she announced. She showed no sign of anything having transpired between us.

She glanced at her watch. An hour until I was out of her life.

"I need to feed the dogs," she said.

I nodded. I knew she would make feeding them take longer than required. I walked to the window. Wet snow lined the sill. My mother was laughing as she fed biscuits to the animals. From a distance, in her motorcycle pants and with her smile, she looked my age.

When she returned to the cabin, she was humming a song I couldn't identify. She used to hum songs no one knew the words to, because she didn't want anyone joining in.

She placed a plate of toast and cheese on the table.

"Olaf will be here soon," she said.

"Can I ask you something?"

She shrugged as she buttered her toast.

"Who was my father?"

Her eye twitched.

"Richard," she said after a moment. Her voice was soft, without its usual edge.

"No," I said. "Who was my father? Richard wasn't my father."

"He told you that?" she said, feigning outrage.

"No," I said. "I met Eero Valkeapää, your first husband."

She put down her bread. "Have you been playing detective?"

"At least I'm fairly positive he was your first husband. Maybe there have been others."

"Did Eero know I was here?"

"No," I said.

A look of disappointment crossed over her face. "He was always so out of it," she said. "But he probably told you the truth. Eero is your real father."

I shook my head. "No, I know what kind of person my real father was." I looked at her hard, and she stared at me. Her expression shifted from disbelief to indignation.

"Do you know who he was?" I asked. For the first time I could remember, I felt stronger than my mother.

She stood up, she sat down. She grabbed the hair at the nape of her neck and released it.

"I did," she said. "That's why I didn't report it. We were all working toward the same goal."

"Protesting the dam."

"Yes." She seemed surprised that I knew. "He was sick in the head," she said as she scratched her neck.

I stared at her.

She took my plate, and I followed her into the kitchen. She turned the faucet on and threw the dishes in the sink with a sudden clatter.

"Please," I said. "Stop cleaning."

She turned off the water. I was surprised.

"So you forgave him?"

"You want to talk about forgiveness?" she said. She faked a laugh. "You probably believe in redemption, too. He did himself enough harm. He tried to blow up a bridge a week after another man tried. He blew off his hand, lost one eye or both. I don't know."

Sweat slid down the backs of my arms.

"An eye for an eye," she whispered, as though it was her own private joke.

"Was he from Kautokeino?"

She nodded.

"Was his mother's name Anna Kristine?"

"I don't know. Some kind of witch doctor."

"Not a witch doctor, a healer," I said.

"Same thing."

My body couldn't have moved if I had willed it to. Anna Kristine had sought me out.

My mother started cleaning again. Forks and knives squealed against the counter. For a moment, she looked so small, so sad. Her motorcycle pants, folded into cuffs at the ankles, were too long for her legs. She lived by herself with eight dogs above the Arctic Circle, on the verge of deafness. I wanted to have known her before the night on the river.

"You poor woman," I said.

"Don't feel sorry for me," she said. "Being patronizing is just a way to make yourself feel better. That's why I left Inari. I was being patronized. I was the woman who was raped. And you were the rape baby. I couldn't do that for the rest of my life. You should be glad I left."

"But how did people know?"

"Even if they didn't know, Eero knew. That was bad enough.

It made him pathetic. His wife raped, and he raises the child. I couldn't look at that kind of man."

I thought of Eero, how much he would have loved me.

"People pretend things didn't happen. Or so what, they happened, it's okay. Well, it's never okay. It's always ruined."

She finished cleaning. She dried her hands on the back of her leather pants. "We're done," she said.

16.

Outside, the headlights of Olaf's approaching snowmobile shuddered across the windows. He was early.

It was over. My time with her was over.

Olaf stomped his feet on the mat outside and stepped in, bringing all the cold of the world.

"How you find it?" he asked.

"I didn't get as much out of it as I had hoped," I said.

"You have to lower your expectations," my mother said.

Olaf made a production of looking uncomfortable. "It is custom to tip Olivia," he said to me.

I searched for what I would leave her. In the bottom of my bag, I found a letter I had composed to the child growing inside me. I had written it after tearing up the first draft. This version was more to the point. *I promise to never disappear*, it said.

I rolled up the letter. As I left the cabin, I handed it to my mother. She would read it later.

"Bye," I said.

"I don't expect you to understand," my mother said.

"Say my name," I said.

"What?"

"Just say it."

She paused and looked not at my nose, but at me. "Good-bye, Clarissa," she said.

17.

We followed the twigs Olaf had speared through the snow. This time, there was no fire, no lingonberry juice. In the near distance, I saw teams of huskies pulling three sleds of tourists. Men, women, and children, dressed in red or blue snowsuits. They waved hello, and I didn't wave back.

18.

Henrik was waiting for me on a bench outside the hotel lobby. He stood when he saw me, as if I was a doctor bringing news.

"Was it her?"

I nodded. *Was Henrik my second cousin? My uncle?*

"How was it?" he asked.

"She didn't ask about my brother," I said. "She's completely forgotten everything."

"The wilderness can do that," he said. He paused. "There are some things that it's better not to know."

The hotel seemed to be melting.

"I'll take you back to Anna Kristine's," Henrik said, proud of himself for offering. He was a boy trying to be a man.

We drove in the afternoon darkness. I pretended I was asleep so I wouldn't have to talk. The closer we got to Kautokeino, the more incensed I grew. Anna Kristine had known who I was, had known who she was to me. In the distance, the lights of Kautokeino shone red. A city on fire.

19.

Anna Kristine greeted us at the door. I nodded perfunctorily and hurried past her to my bedroom. I packed quickly and checked the bus schedule. Nothing that night.

"Are you okay?"

Henrik was standing in the doorway.

"Fine." I refolded a sweater I had already folded and stuffed it into a corner of my suitcase.

"I'm going out and check on the reindeer," he said. "I'll come by tonight. Maybe you want to go to the bar."

I glared at him. "I'm leaving tomorrow."

"I'll drive you to Karasjok so you can get the bus from there. It's easier."

I couldn't force myself to be kind.

"Sorry about your mother," he said. "Sorry it didn't go as you wished."

He was sorry for me; Anna Kristine was sorry for me. Being sorry for someone was a way of saying something wasn't your fault.

He left. I put everything in my suitcase and sat on it to close it. I wanted it to break. To be angry about it breaking. To be angry about something small and ultimately fixable.

20.

Anna Kristine was in the kitchen, preparing dinner. I smelled meat.

I stood in the living room, staring at the door that was blocked by the couch. I knelt on the couch's sagging green cushions and twisted the doorknob. It wouldn't turn.

I got up and tugged the couch away from the wall. It was heavy; its feet scratched the floor. I tried the door again. Locked.

After my mother disappeared, my father locked her belongings in her study. After a year, he moved everything to the storage unit. People took up more space when they were gone.

Anna Kristine was behind me now. She said something in Sami.

"My father's room," I said, and pointed at the door. "My father. Your son," I said, and pointed at her.

She stared at me. If she hadn't been so old, I would have knocked her over. She nodded and stepped out of the room. She and Pankaj were the same, keepers of secrets.

Anna Kristine returned to the room and whispered something to me. Her bony fingers held a key. An ordinary key attached to a short red thread.

21.

Anna Kristine's hand made flat circles on the wall until she found and lifted the switch. Darkness. She left and returned with a flashlight.

I illuminated the room with quick slashes, then focused on one corner at a time. A poster of Saturn, a poster of a squirrel. A screwdriver, a radio, a lamp, a book. A bike helmet on top of a rolltop desk. A dozen pens thrown into a jar shaped like the head of a pig. I held one in my hand. The cap had been chewed raw, as if by an animal.

It was a boy's room, similar to Jeremy's. What had I been hoping to find? Had I really thought that the insane man's room would be littered with terrible writings, with guns and violent collages?

I thought of the missing pictures in Anna Kristine's photo album, the dried glue that framed their absence. I recognized the desire to erase someone. I sat down on the bed, still made neatly, its pillow, small and gray, on the floor. Anna

Kristine sat next to me. She extended her cold hand to mine, and I took it in my palm, her fingers like small branches on a dying tree. I pulled her close to me and kissed the top of her head.

22.

At dinner Henrik told Anna Kristine I was leaving. She spoke in a quick flurry, and Henrik translated.

"She says you are welcome to stay," Henrik said. "She says you can live here if you wish."

No day would pass without a reminder of my father.

"There's nothing I could do here," I offered as explanation. "All the women move to Oslo."

He shrugged and translated for Anna Kristine. She spoke again and he translated. "This is true. And you have your boyfriend or your husband to return to, the father of your child." After Henrik had translated this, he stared at his napkin. "I'm sorry. I didn't know."

"It's okay," I said. "I didn't tell you." I tried to picture Pankaj. Pankaj at the door greeting me. Pankaj at the door forgiving me. I would have to live with that.

I nodded. "Yes," I said. "My fiancé." I could conjure only a Cubist version of his face. His lips here, his eyes there and there.

"What's wrong?" Henrik said.

"Nothing," I said, and turned my attention to my plate. Anna Kristine asked about our trip, and Henrik recounted it in Sami and translated her questions into English. His English grew worse and soon he checked his watch. He stood to clear the table—it was time to go to the bar. The candle had shortened over dinner and I could now see Anna Kristine's face unobstructed. I told myself a lie, that her eyes were like mine.

23.

In the morning Anna Kristine was gone. She had left a pair of small red mittens outside my door, mittens she had knitted for my child.

Henrik came to pick me up, as planned. He had a pink gash across his cheek.

"What's that on your face? The pink mark?"

"Frostbite," he said. "I was wearing a new mask this morning—to see my reindeer. It didn't cover that part."

On the way to Karasjok we talked about his plans for the day. He would sleep, check on his reindeer again, go to the bar. "And you?" he asked. "Back to New York?"

The headlights of an approaching car bounded up like a sunrise.

"I don't think so," I said. I had not been sure until that moment.

We arrived at the bus station and I leaned in to hug Henrik.

"Let's do this properly," he said. We both got out of the car. Henrik lifted my suitcase from the trunk and placed it down between us.

I stepped toward him, removed my glove and raised my hand to his cheek. The frostbitten area was hot. I could feel his heartbeat through my fingers.

"Thank you," I said.

He opened his mouth and closed it again, as though swallowing what he had been about to say. He placed his gloved hand over my bare one, pressing my fingers to his cheek for a moment longer.

24.

From Karasjok, I boarded a bus to Rovanemi. I was relieved I didn't have to pass through Inari, past Eero, again. In Rovanemi, I bought a pack of white stationery and envelopes. "You surprising me not being from here," said the middle-aged woman working at the store. She wore glasses on a chain. "Everyone here is from here."

"My grandmother lives in Kautokeino," I told her.

She nodded, as if she could have guessed as much.

In Rovanemi, I sat inside the train station, my ticket in my hand. It was the same waiting area where I had spent the night almost two weeks before. It looked different now, cleaner, with a poster of Santa Claus on the wall. VISIT SANTALAND, read the caption beneath his wind-chapped face.

I heard the whistle of the train, and moved outside, to the platform. It was a clear day, the ground beneath my boots like buttermilk. I expected to recognize the conductor—I had been on so many trains, seen so many conductors—but he was new. He wore blue gloves and bowed as he took my ticket. "Helsinki," he said.

"*Jå*," I said, nodding.

I sat by the window. As the train picked up speed, we passed a reindeer wandering into a woman's garden. She used a broom to shoo it away.

I dozed into dreams that left me refreshed and wanting more. An hour had passed when I woke for good. We were farther south now, and more houses lined the sides of the tracks. We passed a group of children, all in bright hoods, climbing a hill, dragging red sleds. Their parents stood gathered at the base of the hill, laughing, waving, encouraging.

I surprised myself at that moment by having sympathy for my mother. I didn't forgive her, but I could understand what had possessed her to do what she had done. I was a reminder of her past. She could not look at me without remembering, just as she couldn't look at Eero without feeling like one of his fallen parishioners, someone he was obligated to serve and save. You could not erase a rape—you would always be either victim or survivor. But victimhood requires witnesses, and my mother chose to leave hers behind. Now I was leaving those who knew about me: Anna Kristine, Henrik, Eero.

And Pankaj.

If I returned to Pankaj now, I would be the daughter of a madman. I would be the child of rape, motherless, raised by a quiet man named Richard who Pankaj had always known was not my father. Now Pankaj could not leave me; duty demanded that he stay to care for his wounded bird. I couldn't live with that kind of condescension.

As the train picked up speed, I started a letter to Pankaj.

I decided today that I'm going to stay away for a while. Even as I write this letter I don't know if I'm going to tear it up.

I told him about Eero, about my grandmother, about my mother and the man who had taken her on the river. I told him about Henrik and Kari. I detailed more than he would need or care to know; I wanted it to be impossible for me to return to him. I wanted it to be impossible for him to take me back.

I stood and walked the length of the train. I passed women and men sleeping and children peering into shopping bags. I passed a couple who had fallen asleep holding hands. Their grasp was awkward, like a handshake. Their mouths were both open, as if in shock. I returned to my seat.

I didn't tell Pankaj where I was going. I wasn't sure. I knew that in a few hours I would be in Helsinki, and that from Helsinki I might travel to Amsterdam. But that was all I knew. I didn't know that in Amsterdam, while walking alone amid African tourists and drunken British lads, I would decide to accept the job at the subtitling company in Hong Kong. I didn't know that on the day I arrived in Hong Kong I would be lured into a dressmaking shop by a broad-shouldered woman who would offer me a cold glass of seltzer. That I would leave with three new dresses to accommodate my expanding belly, and that this woman, Allegra, would become my friend.

I didn't know that during the fourth month of my pregnancy I would take a tram up to the top of Victoria Peak, where I would borrow a pair of binoculars from an Australian man so I could make sense of the shapes below. I would end up marrying this man, a gentle and slow-moving man who worked at the embassy. He would know nothing about my past—only that my father was named Richard and that my mother had died when I was fourteen. Together we would raise my daughter in an apartment overlooking the bay. From a young age, we would tell her the truth about her father—that he was a good man, a philosophy professor, that one day she could travel to New York and meet him.

I didn't know that on hot summer days, we would walk down to the beach and swim in the welcoming water. That we would dig holes in the sand, pretending to be digging to America. I didn't know that I would be so successful at becoming someone new. I was not different—I knew who I was and what had happened—but still, in the eyes of my husband and child and everyone I would come to know on the other side of the world, I was neither victim nor the product of an act of violence.

And when I would hear people say that you can't start over, that you cannot escape the past, I would think *You can. You must.* I would go months without thinking of Pankaj, of my father, of the frozen white river where I was made. Sometimes my daughter would pretend her dolls were ill and treat them with various remedies—a warm bath, soup, affection. I would think of Anna Kristine then, and on some nights in bed, in that moment before sleep erased the day, I would picture the way the sky in Lapland looked the morning I left, how the train had sped south beneath a sky that was brighter than it had been in weeks. It had pulsed with reds and oranges, as though hiding a beating heart.

Acknowledgments

I am grateful to the Sami poet Marry Ailoniedia Somby for her poem "Let the Northern Lights Erase Your Name," from which I drew inspiration and a title.

I am indebted to my friends and family in Scandinavia, especially Lars and Mia Wessman, and Linda Saetre, who was an untiring translator and travel companion at an aphotic time of year. Heidi Johansen at the Alta Museum in Norway patiently answered my questions, and the welcoming inhabitants of Kautokeino, Norway, tolerated my inquisitive presence. Thank you also to the ice hotels in Alta and in Jukkasjarvi, Sweden.

My gratitude to my agent, Mary Evans, for her unfailing encouragement, and to my editor, Daniel Halpern, at Ecco, for providing a nurturing home for this book. Also, Carrie Kania, Allison Saltzman, Millicent Bennett, Amy Baker, and everyone else at Ecco: Thank you.

I thank my first readers, Julie Orringer, Lisa Michaels, Sarah Stone, Ron Nyren, Ann Packer, Cornelia Nixon, Ann Cummins, Nancy Johnson, Angela Pneuman, and Eli Horowitz, as well as those who provided invaluable help and input at the end: Sally Willcox, Amanda Eyre Ward, Devin McIntyre, Indu Subaiya, Debby Klein, Karen Duffy, and Vanessa Vida. Thanks also to Paul and Inger Vida, Heidi Julavits, Andrew Leland, Kevin Feeney, and to Galen Strawson, whose essay "Against Narrativity," published in *Ratio*, made me curious about the kind of person who would see their past as unconnected to their present. In trying to answer that question, this novel emerged.

Dedications usually appear at the front of a book, but in this case it seems more appropriate to acknowledge the person who was there from the beginning, all the way through, at the end. D: This book is dedicated to you.

About the author

About the book

Insights,
Interviews
& More...

Read on

Meet Vendela Vida

About the author

Marion Ettlinger

VENDELA VIDA is the author of the critically acclaimed novel *And Now You Can Go* and *Girls on the Verge,* a journalistic study of female initiation rituals. She is the coeditor of *The Believer* magazine, the editor of *The Believer Book of Writers Talking to Writers,* and a founding board member and teacher at 826 Valencia, a nonprofit youth writing lab. Vida lives with her husband and daughter in northern California. ∾

A Conversation with Vendela Vida

How did you first learn about the Sami, and what drew you, as a writer, to them and to Lapland?

My family on my mom's side is Swedish, so I grew up hearing stories about the region. My mom's cousin married a Sami priest, and I remember seeing pictures of him riding into the wedding ceremony on a horse. So the Sami people began to fascinate me from a young age, and their lives had an almost fairy-tale-like power over me. When I finally traveled to Lapland, it was very much like I expected— very little light in the winter, fields of snow, reindeer everywhere—but also very different. I wasn't expecting that the Sami culture would be so vibrant, that I would see people wearing traditional Sami outfits in their everyday lives—in the grocery store, on the bus.

What was the writing process like? How long from inception to completion?

I worked on this book for over three years. I overwrote my first few drafts and then spent a year sculpting the story—the original version of *Let the Northern Lights Erase Your Name* was at least a hundred pages longer than the final book.

Every time I got really stuck in the writing of the book, I would look into trips to Lapland; I knew going back would inspire me again, and luckily, flights to that part of the world aren't very expensive in the dead of winter. ▶

66 Every time I got really stuck in the writing of the book, I would look into trips to Lapland; I knew going back would inspire me again. 99

A Conversation with Vendela Vida
(continued)

*Did anything surprising or unexpected
happen during the writing process?*

There was a moment, during my third trip to
Lapland, when I found myself in the living
room of a ninety-year-old Sami medicine
woman. She was showing me pictures from
her youth, much of which had been spent
herding reindeer. Like many Sami before the
invention of snowmobiles, she had led a very
nomadic life. She was maybe five feet tall and
ninety pounds, but I've never met anyone so
strong, and yet so ethereal. Even while I was
sitting there, petting her dog and eating the
reindeer meat she served, I knew I wanted to
base a character on her. So I created a woman
named Anna Kristine, who ended up having a
larger role in the book than I first intended.
Once she entered the story, the plot took a turn
I hadn't expected, but I liked being surprised
by the influence this very strong and
fascinating woman had on my writing.

*Olivia, Clarissa's mother, doesn't know how
to be a mother, and eventually decides she
doesn't want to be one. How did you come up
with a character like her—kind of an anti-
mother figure?*

To some degree, I created Olivia in reaction to
the mother in my first novel, *And Now You Can
Go*. I love the mother in that novel; I love her
strength and her sense of humor (both of
which I based on characteristics of my own
mother). In many ways, the mother in *And
Now You Can Go* tries to help Ellis, the
protagonist, have greater perspective on the

world, to be less solipsistic. I think a lot of readers liked that mother, and I know for a long time people would say to my mother, "Are you as wonderful as the mother in your daughter's book?" ("Yes," she would answer.)

When I was starting *Let the Northern Lights Erase Your Name,* I knew I wanted to explore motherhood and its legacy through a different lens, with a very different sort of mother. I wanted the mother to disappear one day, and I wanted that disappearance to say something about her. Once I knew this would happen, I became really intrigued: what kind of mother would leave her daughter in a mall and never come back? What would have happened to that mother for her to do such a thing? In trying to answer those questions, I began to think about Olivia as someone who'd experienced a "split" in her life, a defining moment that changed her personality. And that reminded me of a friend I had when I was growing up whose mother had been raped. I'm not sure how my friend found out—she probably overheard conversations—and sometime later, she told me. But we were so young, eight or nine, and we couldn't fully comprehend what *rape* was. We didn't even know what sex was, so how could we understand rape?

Although I was young, I could see a change in my friend's mother after the incident. She wasn't as exuberant, and her laughter, when it came, was very studied and sad. For a long time, I've known I wanted to write about a mother like this, in part to figure out the answers to questions I couldn't ask her when I was young, and would never ask her now. ▶

❝ To some degree, I created Olivia in reaction to the mother in my first novel, *And Now You Can Go.* **❞**

A Conversation with Vendela Vida
(continued)

In your acknowledgments, you mention Galen Strawson's essay "Against Narrativity," which made you curious "about the kind of person who would see their past as unconnected to their future." Can you talk a little more about the influence of that essay on Let the Northern Lights Erase Your Name?

I edited an interview with Galen Strawson, a philosopher, for the first issue of *The Believer*. A year later, I came across an essay he'd written in the *Times Literary Supplement* called "Against Narrativity." It's about how most of us see our lives as a continuing narrative, but there's a small percentage of people who don't view anything they do now as being related to anything that's happened in their past. The essay helped me figure out how Olivia, Clarissa's mother, might be able to compartmentalize her life, how she might leave one life behind completely to begin a new one.

You also mention in the acknowledgments that the title of the novel was inspired by a poem?

Yes, the poem "Let the Northern Lights Erase Your Name" is by a contemporary Sami poet named Marry Ailoniedia Somby whose work I came across when I was in northern Norway. The poem's title seemed to connect so directly with Clarissa's plight—she's searching for the truth of her own identity under the strange sky of Lapland.

> ❝ The essay ["Against Narrativity," by Galen Strawson] helped me figure out how Olivia, Clarissa's mother, might be able to compartmentalize her life, how she might leave one life behind completely to begin a new one. ❞

Clarissa works as a subtitler for foreign films. How important was it to you that her occupation involved making foreign languages accessible to others?

Very important. One of the book's themes (one that I was conscious of, that is) is the difficulty of communication, even between people who love each other. The novel begins with the death of Richard, the man who raised Clarissa, and her discovery that he wasn't her real father; he was so close to her—did so much for her—but never told her the truth. And then there's Pankaj, Clarissa's fiancé, who's been withholding information from her as well. He thinks he's protecting her by keeping a secret from her, but I believe what we don't tell people speaks quite loudly.

I had fun with the fact that Clarissa's job is working as subtitler for foreign films—she's supposed to clean up translated subtitles, and make them more accessible, more accurate. Yet she herself can't even translate or make sense of the events that are transpiring around her.

Clarissa travels to Finland without knowing Finnish, so that obviously provides for a great deal of misunderstanding and unfinished sentences and hand gesturing. But the person she ends up communicating with the best is Anna Kristine, the Sami healer, who doesn't speak a word of English. That was a deliberate choice on my part—to have the apex of communication in the book occur between two people who don't speak a word of the other person's language. ▶

66 That was a deliberate choice on my part—to have the apex of communication in the book occur between two people who don't speak a word of the other person's language. 99

A Conversation with Vendela Vida
(continued)

Do you think, ultimately, Clarissa follows in her mother's footsteps, or does she rewrite history?

That's a good question—and a complicated one. I don't want to give away too much about the ending, but, in some ways, Clarissa does follow in her mother's footsteps (though she's less ruthless than her mother), and in other ways, she breaks away from the cycle of betrayal and parental neglect.

Do you think the decision Clarissa makes is the correct one?

Possibly, possibly not. But I don't think books should prescribe exactly how to live one's life. I'd rather write in a way that raises the questions that might help us decide on a course. I guess I'm more likely to create endings that force the reader to ask questions of themselves than to write a conclusion that ties everything up too neatly.

Do people who know you take Clarissa, the main character, to be an extension of you?

I think we share the same sense of humor—it's difficult to create a character that has a sense of humor different from your own. But I don't think friends who know me would ever confuse us. I'm a pretty outgoing person; I wake up happy and go to sleep happy, whereas Clarissa's a lot more troubled. And she has a right to be confused and angry: her mother abandoned the family when Clarissa was fourteen and her father's just died and she's found out everything she thought she knew about her life is completely apocryphal. My own family story, by contrast, is fairly pedestrian—my parents have been married for almost forty years now.

You have a very minimalist style that, in this book, helps to highlight the things that happen, the interactions between characters, but also shows how mysterious those things are. What are you trying to do stylistically?

I wanted the story to move quickly, to keep up with Clarissa's thoughts, and I wanted the prose to somehow mirror the landscape of Lapland in winter. As odd as it sounds, the words on those white pages look very much like the silhouettes of people moving over the snow of Lapland. I wanted the book to be stark, for the prose to mirror what's happening in Clarissa's life—as she discovers secrets about her family's past, the story of her life becomes more stripped down and laid bare. It seemed incongruent and, well, wrong, to describe what's happening to Clarissa with long, flowing sentences. I didn't think she was someone who would wax poetic about the moon.

You coedit The Believer, *a magazine devoted to reviewing books that might otherwise be ignored and to long conversations with writers, artists, philosophers, directors,* ▶

> 66 As odd as it sounds, the words on those white pages look very much like the silhouettes of people moving over the snow of Lapland. 99

musicians, and inventors. What do you feel your major accomplishments with it are?

My coeditors, Heidi Julavits and Ed Park, were classmates of mine at Columbia. A few years after graduating, we found we missed some of the lively discussions we'd had about books while we were in the MFA program, and we missed being in a community where we could always get recommendations for what to read next. Our goal with *The Believer* (which began publishing every month in 2003) was to bring attention to books published by small presses and to run interviews that, because we're not so limited by space, could really get deeper into the minds of the subject. Also, most magazines face a pressure to be timely; we don't. If someone wants to write at length and with freedom about an unknown book that was published fifty years ago, that's fine with us. The fact that *The Believer* exists at all is something we're all pretty happy about. Our small band of readers has made it possible.

Can you talk a little bit about the classes you teach at 826 Valencia, a nonprofit writing lab for youth that started in San Francisco?

I teach two workshops at 826 Valencia. One is "Writing the College Admissions Essay," which I've taught every fall for the past four years. The other is a year-long foreign literature discussion group called "Found in Translation." We read works by Haruki Murakami, Françoise Sagan, Roberto Bolaño, and lesser-known writers from around the world.

> 66 I teach two workshops at 826 Valencia. One is 'Writing the College Admissions Essay,' which I've taught every fall for the past four years. The other is a year-long foreign literature discussion group called 'Found in Translation.' 99

The college essay class is obviously very practical, but it's rewarding because, come each April, I hear from my students about where they've been accepted. When I was growing up, I didn't have anyone to advise me on the daunting college admissions process— my mother was from Sweden and unfamiliar with American schools, and my father never had the resources to go to college. So I suppose in some way I'm trying to provide guidance that I didn't have.

As for "Found in Translation," foreign literature has always been a passion of mine. At *The Believer*, we've tried to bring the works of foreign writers such as Michel Houellebecq and the Spanish writer Javier Marías to a wider American audience by translating and publishing their works under the Believer Books imprint. I love hearing what my students have to say about the work we read, because they have no preconceptions about what they're "supposed" to think about a particular book or author. They'll tell you all the reasons they love Murakami or hate Proust. At the same time, though, they're incredibly committed to the class. They don't get credit for it at school, and some of the students have to travel pretty far to attend. But I was the same sort of reader in high school, I think—I would have taken three buses to get to a class like that in high school. The great thing about 826 Valencia's evening classes— which are all free and open to any high schooler—is that they bring together really devout readers and writers from all over the city. And these kids, who might not have a peer group at school that wants to talk about ▶

A Conversation with Vendela Vida
(*continued*)

contemporary Arabic or Norwegian fiction, can gather and find birds of their feather. It's a safe haven, really.

Do you see Clarissa as likeable?

Personally, I do. It's funny, because my first group of readers—a group of writer-friends who saw the book before it was published—really liked Clarissa. They thought she was funny and determined, and that she showed great strength and wit in the middle of a very difficult situation. But then the book was published, and occasionally readers would tell me how unlikable they found Clarissa to be. I know that some of that's due to the decisions she makes at the end of the book. But even so, I didn't set out to make an unlikable character; I set out to make her true. I think however you find her—likable, unlikable—you have to take into account that she's a young woman, and you have to consider the extraordinary circumstances she finds herself in. I think she acts with a certain grace, given all that's thrown at her. But if she's not completely likable, that's okay with me, too. Many of my favorite fictional characters aren't perfect—Anna Karenina, Raskolnikov from *Crime and Punishment*, and Humbert Humbert from *Lolita*, to name a few. ∽

Author's Picks

Books Related to Lapland . . .

IN THE SHADOW OF THE MIDNIGHT SUN: CONTEMPORARY SAMI PROSE AND POETRY, EDITED BY HARALD GASKI

Marry Ailoniedia Somby's poem "Let the Northern Lights Erase Your Name" is included in this intriguing collection of short stories and poetry from Swedish, Norwegian, Finnish, and Russian Lapland.

POPULAR MUSIC FROM VITTULA, BY MIKAEL NIEMI

A truly funny and beautifully written coming-of-age novel in which the narrator, Matti, recounts his small-town Arctic Circle upbringing in the 1960s. He describes smells, tastes, and music like someone who's just discovered his senses.

. . . And Other Favorites

DISGRACE, BY J. M. COETZEE

A dark, haunting novel about violence, race, and honor. A literature professor in Cape Town is accused of sexual harassment and escapes to the South African countryside, where he and his daughter become the targets of a more primal sort of crime.

A HEART SO WHITE, BY JAVIER MARÍAS

Javier Marías is a bestseller in his native Spain and elsewhere in Europe, but he remains relatively unknown here. This book, a ▶

Read on

66 [*Popular Music* is] a truly funny and beautifully written coming-of-age novel in which the narrator, Matti, recounts his small-town Arctic Circle upbringing in the 1960s. 99

mystery of sorts, deserves your attention. It starts with a woman killing herself on her honeymoon (through the course of the novel we discover why) and includes playful meditations on prostitution, mistaken identity, and, yes, love.

WHY DID I EVER, BY MARY ROBISON

A blackly funny novel narrated by a quirky scriptwriter named Money, whose daughter is a heroin addict and whose son is the victim of a violent act. Money spends much of her time driving at night (with no particular destination), educating her not-very-intelligent and much-younger boyfriend, and writing letters, all of which she signs "Mrs. Sean Penn."

THE WIND-UP BIRD CHRONICLE, BY HARUKI MURAKAMI

In a kind of reverse *Odyssey*, a Japanese man who spends a lot of time making spaghetti embarks on a journey to find his missing wife. Murakami makes many allusions to Japanese fairy tales, and in some ways, this book reads like one. Murakami is inimitable as a writer—maybe because no one can figure out how it is he creates such magical, potent stories with such simple-seeming language.

A FINE BALANCE, BY ROHINTON MISTRY

Set in India in the mid-seventies, this is a harrowing story of friendship, hardship, and the inequities of the caste system. It's one of three books that's ever made me cry.

" [*A Fine Balance*] is one of three books that's ever made me cry. "

SIAM: OR THE WOMAN WHO SHOT A MAN, BY LILY TUCK

On March 9, 1967, the day the U.S. starts bombing North Vietnam from bases in Thailand, Claire, a young Boston newlywed, arrives in Bangkok with her husband, an American engineer. As people she knows begin disappearing, Claire feels increasingly oppressed and confused. I don't think I'm ruining anything by saying she ends up shooting someone, thereby solidifying the end of her own innocence.